# The Weird, Weird West

## More **Strange Matter**™ from
## Marty M. Engle & Johnny Ray Barnes, Jr.

# The Weird, Weird West

Johnny Ray Barnes, Jr.

**A
MONTAGE
PUBLICATION**

Montage Publications, a Front Line company,
San Diego, California

ISBN 1-56714-055-6

Printed in the U.S.A.

# TO BRAD B.

(so mean, he once shushed a man just for snoring!)

# 1

*Sundown.*

Standing alone in the middle of the dirt street, I watched the horizon. Shimmering waves of heat rippled over the ground, bathed in a hazy, orange glow.

*Something is about to happen.*

Pounds of skin-burning dirt blew past me, obscuring my view of the ball of fire in the sky as it said farewell for the day.

*So did I.*

Laughter. A toothless old man, his face hidden under a matted, grey, spit-covered beard, eyes squeezed into glossy black marbles, rocked in a chair on a store-front porch to my left. The old codger carried on as though he'd seen this a million times before, and knew I had no chance at all.

*Shut up, old man.*

Glimpses of others. Curious townsfolk standing by the side of the road, nothing but shadows in the thick blanket of dirt. I heard more laughter. I heard well-wishes. But I didn't hear anyone offer to help.

Sweat glazed my palms, making them feel heavy and clumsy. My throat was so dry it made swallowing too painful to contemplate. But my eyes stayed clear, focused on the end of the street. Waiting.

*Then he came.*

Emerging through the sheet of dust like a curtain opening, the gunman came forth.

Lit from behind by the setting sun, I saw only a black outline of the man who wanted to kill me—a terrifying silhouette.

Tall. Gangly. He seemed slow. No. Not slow. Precise. He took large, formidable steps. He came closer. Revealing more. He wore tattered rags and a rotted Stetson that stayed affixed to his head, defying the wind.

*Closer.*

There were parts of him that didn't make sense. Parts I could see through. Parts that looked like exposed bone. Pieces hanging from where they shouldn't. The sun shone *through*

2

him. I didn't want him coming any closer.

He stopped.

He held his hands over his guns. Ready.

*Over his guns . . .*

Jutting from the holsters at his sides. Two guns. Two bullets. *For me.*

The wind died. The sun dimmed. The old man stopped laughing.

I heard a voice.

"Draw."

Options tore through my mind.

*Talk it out or run, but do not draw.*

*Do not draw.*

*DO NOT DRAW.*

My hands wouldn't listen. Reaching for my six-shooters, I came up empty. *My holsters were empty!*

I heard explosions from the other end of the street.

I felt something strike my chest—*suddenly my legs turned to jelly.*

I dropped to the ground.

Everything went black.


"Rise and shine, Shane."

Following Pop's voice came the sound of my

blinds being drawn. Sunlight invaded my dark sanctuary and I groaned at its intrusion.

"Get up, son. I've got news."

"School's cancelled? We're taking summer vacation early this year?" I yawned hopefully, opening my eyes to see Pop standing over me, waiting to make sure I was awake.

"There's been an earthquake," he announced.

"An earthquake? Here? In Fairfield? And I slept right through it?" I'd never forgive myself.

"Not here. In Mullinfield. Quite high on the Richter scale, too. Ben Lewis called me this morning. His home's been hit pretty hard." Pop fixed the collar on his golf shirt . . . *golf shirt*? No suit? No tie?

"Aren't you going to work today?" I asked.

Pop winked, grinning slightly. "That's what I wanted to tell you. As his insurance agent, Ben wants me to take a look at the damage. Your mother and I are driving up there today. We'll probably stay for the weekend."

No way.

I shot up, wide awake and itching to see the destruction. "I WANT TO SEE THE EARTH-QUAKE DAMAGE! You're taking me, too . . . *right?*"

"You've got school today, m'boy." Pop's voice took on a serious tone. "Your grades haven't been so hot. Letting you miss school for any reason right now probably isn't a good idea. You're staying here with Grandpa."

GRANDPA?

*Of all the torturous* . . . they can't do this to me. Not for three days. Not seventy-two hours of bad stories, false teeth, pasty food, and whistled snoring. Not Grandpa. Not the woes of pain, the game show participation, or the rolled-cigarette smoking. *Gag, the smoking.*

"Please, Dad," I begged. "Let me come with you. I'll study hard when I get back. I'll make you proud."

"It's a done-deal, son. Grandpa's already here, and we're ready to go." Pop slapped me lightly on the knee, punctuating the end of our conversation.

I hopped out of bed and followed him as he left the room. Mom's hand patted my back as she passed me in the hall.

"You be good and don't give your grandfather any trouble, okay?" She hung her purse over her shoulder, then remembered something. She reached into it and pulled out fifteen dollars.

"This is for the weekend. Don't spend it all at the arcade. And *please* be good." A kiss on the cheek, then, *"Dad,* Shane's up."

"Well, it's about time," a smothered voice strained from the La-Z-Boy. Then it got slightly excited, *"HEY, SHANE-BOY!* We're gonna be roommates, son!"

"Hey, Grandpa," I said, my hopes for viewing the earthquake's aftermath dying at the sight of him.

Grandpa sat in a wrinkled heap in the chair, white hair, big bushy eyebrows, spotted brown-leather skin with a turkey-gobbler throat. He wore a sweater, and a cap that read 'Good Day Tires'. It had been on his head since before I was born. He always steadied himself on his cane, even while watching television, as he was doing just before we walked in. What was on? *The Weather Channel.* Very loud.

"Boy, you're not going to wear your P.J.'s to school are ya? Those little girls won't know what to think . . ." He laughed silently, bouncing up and down, but not making any noise.

Grandpa humor. I wanted to tell him that things had changed a lot since his school days on the prairie. I could wear a kilt to school and no

6

one would look twice. But I decided to chuckle it off instead.

Mom and Pop added a few more things to the List of Things For Me To Do, then bade us *adios*.

"Take care of the house, son," Pop said. "And don't worry, I'll get lots of pictures." He had to, it was his job.

"And don't let Grandpa fall asleep with one of those rotten cigarettes in his mouth. He'll burn himself up!" Mom warned in a harsh whisper.

After a hundred "no problems", Grandpa and I finally convinced them their house would be in good hands, though in Grandpa's case, nervous, old shaky ones. After that, my parents sped off, leaving Grandpa and me to stare at the road in silence for a long moment afterwards.

I looked forward to their return.

I got ready for school quickly. A splash of water on my face, a squirt of toothpaste in my mouth, and even some of Pop's cologne behind my ears. Then, as an afterthought, I decided to leave on my plaid pajama top. Just for Grandpa.

I cruised into the den, heading for the door before Grandpa could stop me with one of his stories. That's when I heard the whistling snore. Looking carefully over at the La-Z-Boy, I saw my elder's head slumped forward, sawing major logs.

Asleep already.

Suddenly he shot back in the seat, eyes still closed, and started to moan.

"MOTLEEEE ... CLAYTON MOTLEY ..."

A name. He cried it out four more times. He was having a nightmare. It sounded like a terrible one.

My skin crawled as I suddenly remembered my own dark dream. Before I awoke, I wanted to cry out just like Grandpa.

"... CLAYTON MOTLEY ..."

Every time he said the name, my heart pumped faster. My veins twisted. My breathing became shallow. I saw the dark silhouette again, felt the bullets slam into my chest.

Who is he?

*Who is Clayton Motley?*

*And do I want to know ... ?*

8

# 2

A light layer of perspiration coated my forehead as I walked quickly to the bus stop. I couldn't think or walk straight, zig-zagging along the sidewalk, scraping against the wall of shrubbery planted just off to the side.

Clayton Motley.

Why did that name scare me so much? Maybe I should've woken Grandpa, and made him tell me what his nightmare was about.

Clayton Motley.

A perfect name for a killer. A perfect name for a shadowy figure standing fifty feet from you with a gun in each hand.

The air around me felt colder, as if it was attempting to freeze my blood.

Clayton Motley . . .

*Something jumped out of the bushes and*

*locked my arm in a death-grip.* My bad arm.

Shocked, scared, *mad*—I reacted. My left hand swung around, and grabbed the thing by its throat and forced it to the ground.

The thing coughed.

"Shane . . . let . . . go . . ."

"When I felt that girlish grip on my arm, I thought it was Rachel Pearson, trying to pay me back for torturing her all those years   But surprise, surprise—it's only you, Gabe."

Gabe Cutshaw. My sidekick. He and I had been getting into trouble together ever since my old partner, Waylon Burst, decided to become a hermit. Yep, Shane Reece and Gabe Cutshaw— the new terrible-twosome. Of course, of the twosome, I'm the most terrible.

"Gonna . . . miss . . . bus . . ." Gabe hacked, his left hand feeling around for the backpack he always carried on his arm, never his back. It lay behind him, just out of reach.

A loud, squeaky bark sounded at the end of the street. Bus brakes. The yellow kid-mover pulled up to the corner bus stop and opened its nice, friendly, *ominous* hatch. I watched the herd of kids pile on. Their cattle-like qualities spawned two physical reactions.

Disgust . . .

"Hey, Gabe, you know what?  Let's not go to school today . . ."

And hunger . . .

"Let's go get a big breakfast instead!"

Gabe's face began to turn crimson.

"Ulp . . . sorry—"

I let him go, and Gabe sat up, gasping for air. His eyes slowly returned to normal size, however his face would remain red for quite some time.

"You could've crushed my larynx.  You could've killed me." Gabe's hands massaged his throat, but it didn't clear his voice up at all. You see, when Gabe talks he sounds like—well, some say Gabe swallowed a joy buzzer when he was younger.  Others say he's half duck.  "I don't want to skip school.  I almost got caught last time."

"Oh come on, Gabey. Doc Shane will just make you another note saying you had to have more throat tests done.  They'll believe that."

"Shut up.  And don't call me Gabey."

"Looks like the bus is leaving . . ." I said, as its doors unfolded and squeaked closed.

My argument wasn't even needed. Gabe always liked to put up a fight every now and then, just to make it look like he had a will of his own.

I noticed something hanging out of his fallen backpack. I instantly recognized what it was.

"Where'd you get the new slingshot?"

Scooping the red marvel from the grass, my eyes studied it like a king holding his favorite diamond. Painted red metal. A wrap-over wrist brace. Rubber tubing instead of a silly rubber-band. *The ultimate weapon . . .*

"I found one of Dad's old ones in the attic, and just customized it a bit . . . ," Gabe explained, but I didn't want to waste any time listening. I had to try this baby out.

Snatching Gabe's shirt, I yanked him into the shrubbery, a natural camouflage. We were perfectly hidden.

"Shane, man—what are you doing?"

Patting the ground for a rock, I came up with a beautiful round stone. It could've said Slingshotrock™ on the side of it.

"Ah, Shane, aw, no—don't do that!"

Loading it into the band, I pulled the stretchy material back, armed and ready for my target.

The big, red stop sign at the corner.

"SHANE ARE YOU CRAZY? DON'T SHOOT AT THE SIGN, YOU'LL HIT THE BUS IF YOU MISS!"

Bustling down the street, the bus' front grill and headlights seemed to form a smiling, innocent face. Its insides stuffed with happy, laughing children, the school bus didn't have a clue as to the disaster about to happen.

But then, neither did I.

Gabe knew not to stop me. I knew I couldn't stop myself. This act would only add to *The Legend of Shane Reece.*

The arm that held back the loaded band started to shake. My bad arm. I know Gabe saw it. And then . . .

The stop sign.

Target sighted.

Fire.

*My hand slipped.*

The rock shot through the shrubs at an upward angle, rocketing over the oncoming bus to smash something in the yard behind it.

Something in *Sheriff Drake's yard.*

The bus drove past, revealing the horror on the other side. The Sheriff's patrol car.

His back window.

Smashed.

"Shaaaaannnnnne—" Gabe got up to run, but I clamped his ankle with my left hand, tripping him up.

"Chill! COOL IT! STAY CALM! No one knows we did this! No one saw us! Let's just cruise away from here and go get some breakfast like I said!" Every time I placed my butt in serious trouble, a rational, sensible Shane Reece invariably shined through. I always wondered where that guy was *before* I got into trouble.

We calmly left the scene, strolling the sidewalks and acting as if we'd never done a bad thing in our lives, and that strolling down the sidewalk while we *should* be in school was perfectly natural.

But Gabe had trouble letting go of the burning guilt . . .

"We're gonna get nailed for this one—" He always got nervous after a stunt. We usually had to get past the first stage of Not Getting Caught—completely leaving the crime scene —before he ever started to settle down.

"We're not going to get caught. I'll spell it out for you, we're *too cool* to get caught."

Gabe loved to have his ego massaged. It

seemed to settle him down a bit. Though his eyes still darted around looking for a screaming adult, he stayed perfectly still when I stuffed the slingshot into his backpack.

"What's happened to your aim? You broke Sheriff Drake's window, and you almost hit the bus!"

I sighed, "It's this stupid arm of mine. My right one. It hasn't been the same since I broke it doing trick dives at the YMCA pool. I've lost my steady shot."

"You'll get it back," Gabe said, knuckling my shoulder.

"Yeah, I hope so."

"Where to?" he asked.

My brain mulled things over. I still wanted a hearty breakfast.

"How about that old western grill, The Steerhunter. Steak and eggs for the both of us!"

Gabe looked at me like I was crazy. "And the money to pay for this is coming from . . .?"

I dug the money out of my pocket and held it in the air with two fingers. "Fifteen bones, my friend!"

Back down the street, someone screamed.

**"NOOOO! WHEN I FIND THE OUTLAW**

**WHO DID THIS, I'LL—"**

*Oh, no.*

Sheriff Drake—I could see him—standing beside his broken car window, arms outstretched, shouting at the top of his lungs.

Gabe and I made tracks.

# 3

*The Steerhunter.*

The sign, topped with bull's horns, said it all. Set atop a building which looked as if it had been lassoed straight from the 1880s. Slightly larger than a saloon, but smaller than a town hotel, the wood-sided beefery served the hungriest of cow-pokes from six in the morning until ten at night. But when the hickory smoke barreled from the chimney, The Steerhunter didn't need a sign saying "open".

Gabe and I climbed the steps to the long wooden porch outside, passing a couple of departing swell-bellied customers prodding their teeth with large, Steerhunter-brand toothpicks. Walking into the establishment, the smokey scent of beef on the grill with onions and peppers assaulted my senses. My nose took an endless whiff, letting the meathouse magic take over my brain and give orders: Mouth—water. Stomach—growl. Legs—grow weak, but move forward.

"You two boys need a seat?"

A waitress, jaws chomping mercilessly on her chewing gum. Her flaming-red hair frizzed-out into a nest of madness, corralled only by the pencils behind her ears.

"Yep," I answered.

"Follow me." The silver palomino earrings in her lobes swung dangerously back and forth as she grabbed two menus from her hostess podium and led us into the dining hall.

A cafeteria for cowboys. Big round tables filled almost every square inch of the room. Half of them were full.

"Big breakfast crowd," Gabe muttered.

What I found funny was how the patronage at The Steerhunter varied. Suited businessmen. Blue-collar working-types. Senior citizens. Two junior high kids. All of them enjoying steak under the same roof.

There was even entertainment. A large overweight man, dressed completely in country-western black (including a black Stetson) sat in a chair on a mini-stage in the corner, tuning his guitar.

The waitress seated us at our table. As I checked the specials on the menu and Gabe slung his backpack over his chair, she pulled one of the pencils from behind her ear to take down our order. I had to ask . . .

"Question. Why do you have *two* pencils behind your ears?"

She smiled, and pulled the other one out to show us. Totally gnarled. Completely chewed on. "I'm on a diet, but working in this beef barn can be tempting. I have to chew on something so I don't pick at the porterhouse. Now *I've* got a question. Why aren't you kids in school?"

Hmmm. Gabe stiffened in his seat. Thousands of stock answers came to mind. I just had to piece and stitch them together to come up with something pure Shane.

"We're from Mullinfield—"

"Oh, my."

"Yeah. My brother and I (Gabe has blonde hair, mine's black.) woke up in the middle of the night with this terrible, well, quaking. It quaked for a long time."

"Uh, huh."

"Well, Dad took pictures of the damage to

show his insurance agent. You see, his insurance agent lives here in Fairfield. Dad's meeting with him right now, so he gave us some money and told us to get some breakfast."

"I see. Who's this insurance agent?"

*She's testing you, Shane. Don't use your dad's name. Traceable. Bluff her.*

"Clayton Motley."

I could see the head of the musician on stage rise when I said the name.

"Clayton Motley? Haven't ever heard of him."

"He just moved to town not too long ago, I think. He works over at the Ronald Reece Agency." *Nice layering, Shane.*

"Oh, I know Ron. A very nice man. So, what will you have?"

She bought it. "The $3.99 Steak-and-Egg Breakfast, please. And a root beer to drink." I didn't even have to look at the menu.

Gabe, however, had his face stuck in his. "I've never seen so many gratuitous, yet succulent, uses for beef. Hmmm. I'll have the Breakfast Beeferito. And make that two root beers."

"My, that's an unusual voice." She scratched down the order. "I'll be right back with those root beers."

Gabe and I sat in silence for a moment, taking in the atmosphere. Loud voices. Hearty laughs. Sounds of a saloon piano coming from the ceiling speakers. All of these elements framing the question Gabe would ask me next.

"Do you think the Sheriff is gonna come after us?"

The waitress left the root beers on the table. I grabbed mine, bent the straw, sucked half of it down, and burped.

"Forget the Sheriff," I said. "He doesn't know anything."

"You've gotten mighty full of yourself since your parents left town." Gabe wanted to analyze me. On our way to The Steerhunter, I'd told him about my parents leaving and putting Grandpa in charge. Now he wanted to use that information to settle me down a bit. "If your grandpa knew what you did today, he'd have a heart attack."

My hand shot over and grabbed Gabe's collar, twisting it.

"But Grandpa's not going to find out, now is he, Gabey?"

Before he could answer, I felt a presence. A

very large one. Gabe's eyes looked from my angry face to *something behind me*, and his mouth dropped open even wider.

# 4

"I'd like a word with you."

The large man with the guitar. The one dressed in black. He stood at our table, looming over us like a dark cloud ready to rumble thunderously. He wore shaded amber glasses, and his face sported a grungy beard with no moustache. His enormous belly actually hung over the table, a fourth participant in our tense group. The man breathed heavily, glazing his lips with moisture from each passing breath.

"Yes?" I chirped. My grip on Gabe's collar became limp and lifeless.

The big man pulled a chair from the next table, where a young businessman started to protest, but then thought better of it when he saw the man's size.

"You spoke the name Clayton Motley," said

the big man. "What do you know about him?" His tone sounded accusing, spiteful. I hadn't made him happy by saying that name.

"I-It's just a name. I made it up." I fidgeted in my seat, my shaky hand clamped itself around my glass, ready to throw it at the monstrous bulk and run. Gabe's nerves were spent. He spilled his root beer in his lap, but was too scared to move.

"No you didn't. It's impossible to make up that name. Where did you hear it?" The chair creaked, almost desperately, under his weight when he leaned in further. His hand wrapped around the glass I held in my grip. He took it, gulped down the rest of my drink, and spit the ice back into the glass.

"I heard my grandpa say it," I said.

"Yeah? What's your grandpa's name?"

"I forget," I said, checking my nerves. Cool exterior. Rationalizing interior. He wouldn't hit a kid. At least not with a whole restaurant full of people around him.

He grinned wide. "Well, not too many people know the story of Clayton Motley. It's one that died a long time ago. But I know it. Your grandpa probably knows it, too. Clayton Motley was a viper. So mean and evil that the great grand-children of those who knew the man still have nightmares about him to this day."

That struck a sharp chord. Nightmares. Grandpa. Me.

I leaned in to hear more. So did Gabe.

"What did he do?" I sheepishly asked. The man eyed us both, possibly considering if he should tell his tale to a couple of kids. I thought that if we were old enough to ask, we were old enough to know. I suppose he thought the same way.

"It's a twisted vine of wickedness, spreading everywhere, but ending right here in Fairfield. Clayton Motley killed men. That was his nature. He killed sons and the sons of sons. His malevolence carried him from town to town, end-ing lives for no gain or purpose. When he came to this town, one man got lucky, and drove the scourge away."

"Who?"

"A man by the name of Nathaniel. I don't know his last name. But he was the one. Everyone else in this town proved to be nothing more than yellow cowards."

*"What did you say?"* asked a hat-wearing-

meat-eating-cowboy from the table next to us. I recognized him. Ernie Johnson, from the farming Johnsons.

"Nothing, son. I'm just telling the boys a story," said the man in black.

Ernie Johnson bounded up out of his seat. "Well I've been listening to your story! You called the Johnsons of past era a bunch of cowards, and I want ya to take it back!"

The man in black slowly got out of his seat, cinching his belt and looking straight into Ernie Johnson's eyes. "Taking it back ain't gonna change nuthin'. I could go back in time and meet your ancestors, change 'em from a bunch of dim-witted, dirt-faced cornhuskers to proud, noble heroes, but it wouldn't change nuthin'. They're still gonna have you, the goofball, dangling off the top limb of the yellow family tree!"

**"THAT'S ALL I CAN TAKE!"** yelled Ernie Johnson, and lunged for the big man, sending his amber shades flying past Gabe's head.

The big man picked up the wooden chair his mass had been torturing and prepared to smash it over Ernie's head.

**"YOU'RE DEAD, FAT MAN!"** The rest of Ernie's table—all Johnsons by some odd link—rose and jumped the big man.

**"I'M TIRED OF THE JOHNSONS THINKING THEY OWN THIS PLACE!"** cursed Retired Admiral Naven Butterfield. From his table behind us, he hopped on top of ours, steadied himself quickly, then leaped into the brawl.

**"OH, YEAH? WELL I'M TIRED OF PEOPLE TAKING SEATS FROM MY TABLE, JUST BECAUSE I'M SITTING BY MYSELF!"** shrieked the young businessman, who bolted out of his chair and headed straight for the man in black. The big man stumbled back, regained his balance, grabbed the squeaking young suit by the neck, and held him, kicking and screaming, six inches off the floor.

*A barroom brawl,* I thought. *Just like on that old show Bonanza—I'd seen them do it a hundred times—but I never thought I'd see one in real life!*

Gabe grabbed his backpack and we ducked under the table as other customers jumped from their seats, announced a basis for hostility, and began pushing their neighbors. We looked for a way through the chaos. Every opening was soon filled by the brawl, which sounded like billiard balls colliding on an endless break.

My eyes caught sight of a narrow path to the door. Signaling Gabe to follow, I began crawling across the battlefield.

Food and plates fell to the floor like rain as we tracked our way through. Retired Admiral Butterfield grabbed onto Maynard Johnson, who had broken the Admiral's daughter's heart a year before, and wouldn't let go. Mailman Forrest Diggs became a human rocket as Big Bubba Johnson spun him around like a sack, then launched him into the air, to land on the cart carrying my steak-and-egg breakfast. Then I saw the man in black pick the young businessman up over his head, and hold him like a broomstick behind his neck. Ernie Johnson had recovered from his bashing, and he and his brothers had regrouped, rushing for the big man. The man in black spun the young businessman around, knocking the stampeding Johnsons to the floor.

*Unreal.* I kept a sharp eye on the battle, but my arms and legs kept moving, inching me toward the door. When I got to the entrance, my hand felt a cold leather shoe.

I looked up.

*Oh, no.*

Sheriff Drake.

He held a police bull horn up his mouth and bellowed, **"ALL RIGHT PEOPLE, THAT WILL BE QUITE ENOUGH!"**

Every soul in the restaurant froze.

The Sheriff eyed the lot of them, inspecting the injury and destruction a few crazy moments had brought to The Steerhunter.

"I can't take all of you downtown," the Sheriff announced. "So I'll begin with the troublemakers. Who started all of this?"

Again, silence.

Then the gum-chewing waitress emerged from the back, pulling eggs from her scattered red mane.

"There wasn't any trouble until those two Mullinfield boys showed up!" she ratted, and pointed straight at us.

"Mullinfield boys?" The Sheriff looked down at Gabe and me, covered in brawl stuff and trying to look as innocent as possible. "Shane Reece. And his sidekick, Gabey Cutshaw."

"Gabe."

"Cutting school are we? Well, that's breaking the law. And boys, people who break the law in my town go directly to jail!"

# 5

A blanket covered the shattered back window of the squad car. For a moment, I sweated it out, wondering if the Sheriff knew it was me who did it. Then I calmed down, reminding myself that the Sheriff had never been known for his sleuthing abilities. His son, Russell, who lived for a good mystery, would probably guess the culprit before his dad did.

Gabe punched me in the arm, yanking my brain back into the here and now. In the back seat of a police car. On our way to jail.

Gabe's face cursed me silently, his mouth forming words his mother would scold him for using. But we rode in silence except for the periodic transactions between the Sheriff and his police radio. My stomach twisted with every turn that brought us closer to the police station.

We'd really blown it this time.

*I'd really blown it.*

"Inside, son," the Sheriff said, leading me into the small, cement-walled cubicle that looked as barren as a desert. A jail cell. It had come to this. Trudging to the center of the cage, I turned to the Sheriff.

"Don't I get a phone call?"

He slammed the barred door, locking it with his key. "Son, you don't need to be spouting that TV stuff to me. I know your number. I'll call your folks." He held a whimpering Gabe with his other hand. When they disappeared into the next cell, my sidekick's sobs turned into outright cries.

"I WON'T DO IT AGAIN! PLEASE DON'T PUT ME IN JAIL! DON'T CALL MY PAR-ENTS! I WON'T DO IT AGAIN! I PROMISE!"

"You've broken the law, son. You're in it even worse than your friend! I found a slingshot hanging out of your backpack! You've got to be at least eighteen years old to have one of those things. You could hurt somebody, or bust a window, or something. Now quiet down and deal with the consequences! I'm calling your mom and dad!"

"NOOOOOOOOOOO—"

Gabe's howling went on for minutes, dying off only when Sheriff Drake threatened him with a pointed finger. I couldn't blame him for crying, though. His parents were going to kill him.

*Your parents are going to kill you, too, Shane,* my little voice warned.

Oh. Oh, man. I had blocked the idea out of my head. Instead, I thought about the crowd that would form around me on Monday and listen to my story. I never once let myself think about the trouble I would be in.

*This is the worst thing you've ever done, Shane,* my little voice spoke again. *Your parents will give you the punishment of a lifetime . . . when they get back.*

That's right. They're gone. When Sheriff Drake rings my house, the only person he'll get is . . . Grandpa.

I almost laughed when I envisioned the phone ringing at my house and Grandpa scuttling over to answer it. Of course, once he knew what I had done, I couldn't imagine what might happen next. He might forget about me and fall back asleep on the La-Z-Boy. Or he might risk his life, as well as others, and get behind the wheel—a geriatric spitfire racing to save his kin from the evil Sheriff.  Or he may just start the long walk to come pick me up, and simply get lost.

*Ugh, the possibilities were limitless.*

I couldn't think about it.  Gabe's cries for mercy and calls for my death made a pin cushion out of my brain.  Lying down on a hardwood bench disguised as a cot,  I watched the last working fluorescent light flicker above me, saying its last goodbyes.

Flicker.

Flicker.

Out.


The orange haze again.  The cackling old man.  Scared townsfolk scurrying from the streets.

I stood in the same place, shaking violently because this time, I knew my situation.

*Target practice for Clayton Motley. An addition to his monstrous body count.*

Scanning the blowing dirt for the killer, my heart screamed to my mind—*there's hope! Stay calm! Think!*  My brain searched for an answer.

Suddenly, what at first appeared to be a fluttering sand shadow, became a familiar, twisted outline approaching through the small desert hurricane.

*Motley.*

My brain quickly delivered an answer.

*Run.*

I listened. Spinning around, I high-tailed it in the other direction. My spurs jingled with every cowardly step, my hat leapt from my pathetic yellow head.

*I don't care. At least I'll be alive.*

Behind me, two shots rang out.

Two bullets zipped into my back, arching my spine so my eyes looked up at the sky. My feet got tangled up, spinning me around and dropping me to the ground like a puppet. I landed on my back, numbed by the two searing chunks of lead inside me, and watched the clouds and sky dim.

A rotted gunman, half man and half skeleton, appeared above me. He held two smoking guns and wore a raggedy, brown Stetson.

"Motley," I uttered with my very last breath.

Then, blackness.

"Wake up, boy. Dream time's over."

Grandpa.

My eyes snapped open to find him standing at the cell door, staring at me with a cold look.

"Grandpa? Grandpa, listen. I'm sorry—"

His hand shot up in the air, warning me not to say another word.

"Let's go home," he said in a tone I'd never heard from him before. Serious. Unforgiving.

It scared me.

# 6

Grandpa drove us home carefully in his '84 Lincoln Towne Car—as clean as the day he bought it. Not one traffic law was broken on the way home, and not a word was spoken.

When we reached my house, we silently got out of the car. Grandpa unlocked the front door and we went in. He hung up his jacket, but kept on his hat as usual.

Then, without turning to look at me, he said, "Take out the trash."

I watched him for a second, expecting more orders or comments, but none came. Going to the kitchen, I slid open the trash compactor and cinched up the garbage bag, cringing at the drops that leaked from the bottom. Rushing it out of the house, I dropped it at the regular spot on the sidewalk. Just in time, too. I could see the garbage truck coming down the street. A light load for them this week from the Reece home. We usually have three or four bags. Today it was just one.

*Unless I didn't get all the trash.*

Groaning, I rocketed back inside. Turning into the kitchen, I checked the Things To Do List stuck to the refrigerator.

## 1.  TAKE OUT <u>ALL</u> OF THE TRASH.

*Groan again.*

Now I understood Grandpa's method. My punishment, for starters at least, would be completing the entire Things To Do List. Which meant taking out *all* the trash. Which meant I only had seconds.

Storming through the house, I emptied every tiny trash can, picked up every bit of miscellaneous junk, and filled two large trash cans. I bolted out the door with them just as the garbage truck pulled away from my house.

I chased it down the street. Cody Cutshaw, a Fairfield garbage man and Gabe's cousin, hung on to the back of the truck and laughed at me the whole way. When the truck finally stopped, he got the heaviest bag in the gut.

When I got back to the house, Grandpa had the television tuned to *Name That Price*.

*And the item is—feta cheese. Half a pound. Is it $2.50, $3.00, or $3.50?*

"THREE DOLLARS! THREE DOLLARS! TWO-FIFTY'S TOO LOW, BUT YOU NEVER PAY MORE THAN THREE FOR FETA CHEESE!"

A compromising moment for Grandpa. We'd have to laugh about this one together.

But instead, he saw me and said, "The dishes."

And so the day went. I worked through every item on the list, a whole weekend's worth of work in one day while Grandpa sat through a myriad of afternoon programming. As the sun set, I mowed the final row of grass in the front yard, switched off the lawnmower, and pulled it into the garage like a sack of rocks.

Grandpa waited for me on the porch, two frosted root beers in his hands.

"Here," he said, his shaky mitt offering me carbonated bliss. I grabbed it and collapsed into a porch chair, chugging half of the bottle before finally sitting back.

"I brought the candy jar out, too," he said, holding up a rainbow of sweetness dropped into one glass container. My hand dug inside and came up with, *mmm, Jolly Rancher.*

Grandpa eased his way into the other chair, and pulled his tobacco from his pocket.

Oh, boy. Here it comes.

*Smelly tobacco.*

He pulled a cigarette paper from his pocket, scattered some of the tobacco leaves on it, rolled it, and lit it. A second later, he was puffing away.

"Tell me something, boy," Grandpa said after swigging a taste of root beer. "Why do you act so crazy? Don't you get enough surprises out of life?"

"It's not the surprises, Grandpa. It's the fame. I want everyone in Fairfield to know the name Shane Reece. I want to become a legend. That's why I do all that stuff, I guess."

Grandpa swigged again, coming up with a different taste this time judging from his cringe. "Well, I think after today, you won't have to worry about that."

"Are you going to tell Mom and Pop?" I asked softly, letting the question ripple gently across the air, testing it.

"Of course. And if I didn't, they'd hear about it from some neighbor. You know that."

True. My subdivision, Forest Oaks, bred gossip. My parents would know before they even hit the driveway. Grandpa knew it, too. Pretty smart of him. "I'm sorry, Grandpa. For pulling this while you're here."

"It doesn't matter if it's me, or your mom and pop. That tomfoolery is gonna get you into something deep! You've got to take responsibility for your own actions, y'know? Or else, yer nothing better than a criminal. And not even a good one at that. Yer stealing respect away from others, and yer not even keeping any of it for yerself. Y'know what that gets ya? Nuthin'. In short, m'boy, grow up."

*Oh, the words . . . the words!* The very words I knew would be spoken to me someday, but I never would have guessed from Grandpa. Which made me think, *if I dreaded hearing them so much, then they must hold some truth.*

We sat in silence for a few more moments. Grandpa puffed away on his stink-stick as the sun took one last glimpse over Fairfield.

"I heard what you said while you were

asleep in that cell. You said *Motley*."

My heart jumped at the name. "Yeah. You said it, too. This morning when you were sleeping. You were having a bad dream and said his name!"

Smoke jettisoned from Grandpa's nostrils. He rocked slightly, trying to cover the fact that he was trembling. "Do you know who he was?"

"A gunfighter. A killer. He terrorized towns all over the world. Until he came to Fairfield. Then a guy named Nathaniel shot him."

"That's right," muttered Grandpa. "Nathaniel Reece."

What?

A psychological brick fell to earth, crashing into my brain. My jaw dropped like a rock.

"Is he one of us?" I managed to ask, only half intelligently.

"He's your great, great, great, great grandfather. And he got very, very lucky. It was a known fact back then, and in certain circles today, that Nathaniel Reece couldn't hit the broad side of a barn with a bullet. Much less out-gun Clayton Motley. But he had something on his side that day. He met Clayton out in the middle of the street over beside Blood Creek, where Blood Creek Highway runs today. They faced each other down, and Nathaniel fired a crazy shot that defied the laws of physics. It flew around and blasted Clayton Motley in the hind side. Then, Clayton's two henchmen came out looking for revenge, and Nathaniel shot them, too. Something had definitely turned Great, Great Grandpappy's gun into gold. But his victory was short-lived. Somehow, someway, Clayton escaped."

"Escaped?"

"Yep. They sent a posse after him, but he was never found. He disappeared without a trace."

"And no one ever heard anything?"

"He had no last words. No grand declarations to the town. But there were rumors. Whispers from Fairfield's underbelly. Dark stories shared only in shadowed corners. Those were Clayton's words. They spoke for him better than he could himself."

"What did they say?"

"That he was coming back. That no one could kill him. And when he returned to Fairfield, he would burn it down and catch its falling ashes in his mouth like flakes of snow.

He would bury the rubble, and not even leave a marker as to what a worthless town it was. But that's only after—"

He snubbed out his smoke, casting the last of the poison from his lungs.

"After what?"

Grandpa held another to his mouth, already rolled, but stopped to say . . .

"That's only after he found every living Reece *and gunned them down.* Only then, could he let himself enjoy life."

# 7

That night, I couldn't sleep.

My bed cried for me to lie down, but my nerves refused, opting instead to have me circle my room as many times as possible, pacing back and forth, casting glances out the window at each pass.

Expecting to see Clayton Motley staring in.

*He's been dead for years. Three or four lifetimes, at least.*

Little comfort. The image I saw in my dreams was almost as terrifying as seeing him in real life.

Passing the window again, I stopped and peered out.

The hill on the edge of our neighborhood—the Lookout, we called it—served as a hangout for Gabe, me, and Waylon (when he came out of the house). Our spot was on top. A light, twinkling softly in the night haze, shone from that same spot. *Someone was up there.*

Since Waylon became a hermit, the only people who go up there are Gabe and I. And once, we did talk about using flashlights to signal the other for a night meeting.

Maybe it *was* Gabe.

Maybe he wanted to tell me about each level of what I was sure was a twelve-step punishment for our escapades earlier in the day.

And the flickering did look like a signal.

In true Shane Reece form, I climbed out my window and headed for the hill.

A very cold night. It felt like a layer of ice covered my skin. Seasons may change, but the nights in Fairfield are always cold. Hunching my shoulders in a vain attempt to warm my neck, I thought about Gabe and getting this little rendezvous over with as quickly as possible. Instead of using the streets, I cut through various yards to shave off the distance.

When I reached the hill, I quickly realized that in order to climb it, I'd have to pull my hands from my pockets. Groan. Halfway up the hill, they were already chapped. But when I finally reached the top of the hill, the answer to my prayers awaited me.

*A campfire.*

So that's where the light came from. Nice and contained, a perfect campsite fire. Good man, Gabe. Of course, if Sheriff Drake were to see this burning, he'd surely come and investigate. I guess Gabe was willing to take that chance.

"Gabey?"

No answer. Maybe he went to get more wood for the fire or something. *Well, I suppose I'll just wait . . .*

Moving to the fire, I held out my chilled hands for defrosting. The fire snapped and crackled, almost as a greeting. The heat soothed the standing hairs on my arms, and washed over my numbed nose.

I heard something snap.

"Gabey?"

Mysteries ended only as far as the light touched, but beyond that, in the blackness, I was certain many things remained hidden.

I wanted to see Gabe now. More than ever.

Another snap.

The fire, though a nice size, couldn't keep me warm anymore. I felt weak. All of my blood washed to my throat and thumped there. The rest of my body just housed the bones, useless parts with no purpose but to crumble.

"Gabe?"

Nothing.

*More than enough of a chance for you to show up, pal. I'm out of here.*

Turning around, I saw a white figure at the edge of the clearing.

*Glowing white.*

My throat managed a squeak.

*It started coming toward me.*

*Not walking.*

*Not running.*

*Floating.*

*It didn't scream.*
*It didn't cackle.*

The glowing figure glided silently over to me, growing more distinct as it approached. It lowered itself to the ground, staring me in the face. Its eyes were totally black—a glossy texture with no white in them at all, and no pupils to speak of. A blood-red wash coated the inside of its mouth, its yellow teeth clamped down hard at the sight of my terror. Painted skin, a glistening electric blue as if it bathed itself in a pinch of daylight sky, punctuated its deathly, immediate presence out of the fluttering firelight.

But I didn't want to look at it anymore. I didn't want to notice the derby it wore on its head, or the watch swinging from its vest pocket, the ticking growing louder and louder. I just wanted to pass out, or have it leave, or wake up from another ghostly dream.

I never wanted it to speak to me.

*"He's coming."*

My lungs searched for the air to answer. Perhaps not to question, but to scream. My legs had finally had enough. They folded, and I found myself crashing to the ground next to the fire.

*"Clayton Motley is alive and he's on his way to this town. To kill the Reeces."*

The flames beside me began to change. A different hue. Green. The transformation made the campfire cough, its fiery tongues lashing out at me. I rolled out of the way, fixing my eyes back on the spectre, which followed me to my new spot.

*"Nathaniel Reece was not lucky. Nathaniel Reece had a supernatural power loaded into his gun. Special bullets, forged from a very special metal. This is the only thing that let him win that day, but it came with a curse. It also kept Clayton Motley alive."*

The spectre's words never matched its moving mouth, but its sentences rang in my head. *This was total madness. Clayton Motley was dead!* I grabbed a rock and shot it at the floating terror. The missile passed right through it, and the glowing nightmare never once slowed his speech.

*"He was no threat until this morning. He had hidden from the posse in a cavern just outside Mullinfield, where a cave-in trapped him. There he would have died, if it wasn't for the strange poison pumping through his veins. Poison from the strange bullet. He passed over death, and began to rot. And there he's lived for over a hundred years, preserved in part by the cave's gases, scratching and clawing at the rock to get out. Until the earthquake there this morning. It freed him from his prison. And he has only two things on his mind. Fairfield. Reece. He will do whatever it takes to get here. Vengeance and the unknown fuel his mission. You don't have much time."*

"W-What do I do?"

*"The strange alloy the bullets were made from. The poison that keeps him alive. Too much of it and he will sour, killing him once and for all. I know this . . . now. You must*

*give him more of it. Even the slightest amount will burn his bones and leave him with no foundation."*

"I don't know—"

*"His two partners. They were shot with the same gun. They died and were buried here in Fairfield. Pull the bullets from them."*

"Where?"

The spectre turned.

A light from the side of the hill, climbing up.

*Someone was coming!*

Before my eyes, the glowing spectre faded away, and the green hue of the fire returned to its natural state.

*Hide!* My brain screamed—and I did, diving behind a fallen tree, landing in a puddle of muck.

Peeking over the trunk, I saw Sheriff Drake top the hill.

I shot back down and didn't move. If the Sheriff caught me here it would be off to a maximum-security prison, I was sure.

I remained hidden until the Sheriff put out

the fire, searched the area, and finally left.

I stayed behind the tree trunk for a few long moments, waiting to see if the spectre would return, trying to calm myself down and keep my teeth from chattering.

Nothing ever came.

I crept away, returning home to a night that I knew would remain sleepless.

**9**

*A dream.*

That's what I believed when I awoke the next morning. Nothing but a dream. Another bad one, but a dream nevertheless.

But when I found my muck-soaked blue jeans hanging out from under my bed, I knew I couldn't deny it anymore.

*It had happened. The spectre. The story. Clayton Motley.*

It was all true . . .

*If the story was true, my only hope was to find the two buried partners. But where? The spook didn't tell me. How could I find out?*

My brain answered, *duh, dummy. Who told you about the two partners in the first place?*

Grandpa.

"What did ya do to yer hand?" Grandpa

piled some eggs on a plate then garnished them with two slices of bacon. Lightly-toasted bread popped from the toaster as Grandpa pulled a pot of coffee off the stove. On television, *The Weather Channel* meteorologist praised the day as one of the most beautiful yet for the year.

"Morning. Sit down and I'll make you a plate." He poured the coffee into his old metal thermos.

"Why do you drink coffee out of that thermos, Grandpa?"

Grandpa stopped sipping and glanced at his container. "I had this here thermos when I was a salesman. I could never keep my coffee warm as I went from door to door, so your grandma gave me this, bless her soul. I consider it my lucky thermos."

Hmmm . . .

"Grandpa, remember yesterday when you were telling me about Clayton Motley's two partners, and how your grandfather put 'em down?"

"Yep."

"Well, where did they bury those guys? Here in Fairfield? Was it near Blood Creek?"

Grandpa chewed his eggs, thinking about the question.

"Nope. Not at Blood Creek. Soil's too moist, the caskets would just shoot up out of the ground." He made a surfacing action with his hands. "No. I don't know where they buried those fellers, but it probably wasn't the purdiest of places."

Great. Now I only had one other option—short of getting another supernatural visit from the spectre to finish his stinking story.

The man in black. The big man. The scary guy from The Steerhunter. He's the only other person who had any knowledge of Clayton Motley.

But returning to that grill would be suicide.

Grandpa's shaky hands raised the thermos to his mouth as he watched the televised weather forecast, fascinated. He connected with those reports. Soaring with the highs, dipping with the lows, Grandpa's was a simple, happy life. If what the spectre said was true, Clayton Motley would end that happiness.

*Unless I did something.*

Grandpa wouldn't have a chance against a monster like that. But I'm young. I'm quick. I might be just lucky enough just to pull it off. Even if it meant risking a whole summer's worth of punishment, I had to return to The Steerhunter and find the man in black.

"So Grandpa, what's on my agenda for today?" Whatever he had planned, I somehow had to slyly get out of it.

"Nothing. Have fun. When your parents get back, they're going to punish you enough. You might as well make the best of what little freedom you've got left." His trembling hand tipped his thermos to his mouth, pouring the last of the coffee down his throat.

*I may be locked in my room for the rest of my life,* I thought, *but I'd gladly serve that time to see Mom and Pop come through the door right now.*

# 10

I didn't think about what my first words to Gabe might be.

His punishment was probably quite severe. And, considering how furious he was with me the day before, he had probably changed allegiances. Now, for the next couple of months at least, he would be the perfect son. An idea I used to see as pretty gooberish.

That's exactly why I acted now. Clayton Motley was coming after the Reece family. The only one in town who could stop him was me. But I needed help.

Gabe, no matter how mad at me he might be, seemed the logical choice.

I crept behind the tall hedges that bordered his yard. Gabe's folks had him mowing the grass, the longest of his Saturday chores. A purposeful torture, since you get to see all of your friends riding their bikes through the streets while you have to walk a noisy, smelly machine around your yard for an hour. Poor kid.

I knew if his parents saw me, my skin would be hanging from their wind chimes. Of course, Gabe couldn't hear me call his name with the mower on. *Which meant I'd have to throw something at him.*

Dirt clod.

I'd grown up with dirt clods, earning stripes in roof-bombing, car-bashing, and head-smacking. But now I felt the cakey wad quiver in my hand. The bad one. Summoning all the confidence I could muster, I let the projectile fly, zooming over Gabe's head and exploding on top of his father's freshly-washed Mercury Cougar.

Gabe spun around, his eyes wide. His look saying at first—I'M DEAD!—but then—YOU!

I waved.

Gabe's searing expression didn't look hopeful, but he glanced over to his front door to check for his parents, then pushed the mower toward me. Leaving it in an easy-to-get-to-if-Dad-walks-out spot, he crammed his head through the shrubs to speak to me.

"I can't believe you! What are you gonna do now? Throw me under the mower?" His eyes searched for some kind of reasoning in my face.

I'd gone way beyond reason.

I explained the situation in less than thirty seconds, a risky amount of time considering his parents' regular patrol. His look twisted to new contortions of disbelief. Before I even finished, he was shaking his head.

"You're loony," he exclaimed.

"No, I'm not. I'm as serious as I've ever been, and I know you're the only one who will believe me. I need help!"

"Shane, you're seeing ghosts! You're telling me that you met a spectre on a hill, and that it told you all of this crazy stuff! You're going to take ghosts at their word?"

"I have to. If I don't do something, no one will! And remember, when I go down, Fairfield goes next! Try explaining that one to your parents! You think you're in trouble now? Explain to them that you could have stopped the town from being destroyed, but instead, you mowed the grass! Man, *they'll be so mad at you . . .*"

That hit Gabe where he lived. Like most kids, he feared his parents' wrath more than anything else. Not to mention, he could never resist the urge to believe even my wildest rantings.

"What do you want me to do?" he asked.

"Be my partner. My sidekick!"

Gabe shook his head. Not good enough. "Deputy."

"Okay. Deputy. Now, let's go," I said.

"Go? Where?"

"The Steerhunter."

**"NO!"**

A web of negotiations followed. Promises and verbal treaties between Gabe and his parents while I hid safely outside. They approved an unchaperoned two-hour library visit. Another thirty minutes got tacked on for him to pick up a few things at the grocery store. Finally, in a surprising move, Gabe got himself another hour for a museum visit so he could earn extra credit at school.

Of course, none of this would get done, and he was only digging himself in deeper. Once you start lying, it all goes downhill from there.

But he wouldn't do it unless somewhere deep inside, he believed me.

And I believed the ghost.

I couldn't decide which one of us was crazier.

## II

We stopped at the edge of the steps leading to The Steerhunter.

I looked at Gabe. He was a trembling ball of nerves.

"They're probably not going to be too friendly to us in there, so here's what we're going to do: we're going to walk in there like we own the place. I'm going to have a few words with that big guitar man, and then we're going to stroll out of there calm, cool, and collected. Got it?"

Gabe's voice squeaked. His head nodded.

We went up the steps, through the doors, and up to the hostess podium. A woman with short brown hair smiled at us as we entered. Obviously, she didn't know us.

"Will it be just the two of you, today?" she asked.

"No, thank you," I replied. "We won't be eating today. I'm looking for the musician who was in here yesterday. Big man, dressed in black?"

The lady shook her head. "No, I don't know him, but that's not surprising. I just started today. I'm sorry."

Gabe grabbed my arm to leave, but I stood firm, looking into the restaurant. "Is the hostess with the red hair here today?"

"Marian? Oh, yes. She's working behind the counter today!" the smiling hostess said.

"We'll just go have a soda, then." I said, and mosied on in.

The piano music blaring from the speaker, just like the day before, stopped.

All of the patrons turned and stared at us.

I shook my head. I had that deja vu feeling again, like I was in a scene from an old western movie.

Retired Admiral Butterfield, the young businessman, and a whole table full of Johnsons watched in silence as we came in.

Gabe and I bellied up to the counter. Marian had just set down a customer's steaming plate of beef and noodles when she saw us sit down. Her expression said it all.

"I thought the Sheriff told you two to never come in here again," she said.

"Give me a root beer," I shot back, slapping a buck on the table.

"Two," said Gabe, signaling me to throw down some more cash.

She grabbed two glasses, poured, and slid the drinks in front of us.

I chugged mine down and set the glass in front of me. "I'm looking for the big fat musician who was tuning his guitar in here yesterday. Do you know where he is?"

She started to wipe off the counter, then stopped. "Mully Sheppard? He's only in town for the weekend. I guess he's over at the Lonestar Hotel. That's where he usually stays."

Mully Sheppard. Typical Country-Western-Cowboy-Wanna-Be name.

"Would he be there now?" I asked.

"I don't know. Maybe. I'm not his personal secretary." She looked at the money on the counter. "That'll be four dollars for the drinks. Two bucks each."

"WHAT?" Gabe guffawed. "A two-liter bottle of that stuff's not even a dollar!"

"Well you didn't buy the bottle, now did

you?" She looked me in the eyes. "You—you're not gonna start any trouble, now are you . . .?"

I slammed another dollar on the counter.

"Give me the bottle!" I said in my best John Wayne voice.

With fear in her eyes, Marian reached under the counter, pulled out the whole bottle of Goodboy Root Beer, and slid it my way.

Never taking my eyes from her, I twisted the cap off, then turned it up. Out of the corner of my eye, I could see Gabe fidgeting nervously while I downed the first liter. It scorched my throat. Carbonated bubbles popped up into my nose and under my eyes, but I couldn't stop. The entire grill was watching. The last few swallows were a lesson in pain. The final drops passing my lips, I brought the bottle down, slamming it to the counter.

Marian's jaw dropped as she stared at me.

Gabe leaned over to look at my face.

I just gazed into space.

Something . . . something was wrong.

"Shane," Gabe whispered. "Are you all right?"

I turned to him, my eyes filling with tears. "I—I can't burp!"

A roar of laughter filled the restaurant. Marian almost fell over backwards, cackling at my gastronomical dilemma.

"GET ON OUT OF HERE!" she cried. "RUN HOME TO YOUR MOMMY AND DADDY! I'M SURE THEY'LL PUNISH YOU GOOD WHEN THEY FIND OUT YOU CAME BACK HERE!"

Gabe helped me off the stool, and eased me through the giggling beef-eaters—who pelted us with wadded-up napkins as we hurried out the door.

Once outside, Gabe looked me in the eye. "Are you all right?" he asked.

I held my cramping sides, my fists massaging the huge air bubble in my gut. "I have to be," I choked. "We've got to get to the Lonestar Hotel. Mully Sheppard's got some talking to do."

# 12

The lobby of the Lonestar Hotel looked undesirable at best. Dust painted the air. At first glance, its circulation seemed to be the only thing in motion. Then I saw the hotel registrar's hand slip from under his chin and his sleeping head crashed to the counter.

Gabe and I walked over.

"We're looking for Mully Sheppard," I said. "We were told he could be found here."

The bald, droopy-eyed counter jockey straightened up, shook the sleep from his head, and responded reflexively, "Mully Sheppard? I don't believe we have a Mully Sheppard . . ." He started flipping through his books, obviously lying.

"Look," Gabe said. "We're kids. There's no way you're going to get a bribe from a kid."

The counter man stopped looking. "Nope. No Mully Sheppard here."

I laid five dollars on his book.

"Ah, yes. I'm sorry. Mully Sheppard? Right through those doors and to your left."

"You're really pathetic, you know that?" Gabe grumbled to the man who was already double-hand snapping his new five-dollar bill.

We walked into a hall where the dust turned into smoke and the lights were dimmed to uselessness. Taking the first left, we stepped into a large dining room, a shrine to the Lonestar's glory days. A rotted upright piano sat in the corner. A stage next to it was framed with burnt-out light bulbs. Dining tables covered the floor, all of them empty. Except one. In the far corner sat Mully Sheppard along with two other men. They were engaged in . . . oh, boy . . . a card game.

Gabe and I walked over.

"On your toes, boys, it's the outlaws," Mully joked as we came into the light of the small lamp hanging above them.

"We've come for some information," I said, growing tense already.

Mully looked like he was in complete control.

Even the chips were piled on his side. "Well, I don't want to be rude. Boys, my fellow players here are John Cratchett, the town mortician, and Lloyd Phillips, the town barber. Lloyd, you've probably trimmed their locks before, huh? And John, they haven't needed you yet!"

"I don't believe I've ever seen these two in my shop before," the old grey-sideburned barber said.

"I go to the Hair Conquistador," I said.

"Ah. *Where bad hair is overthrown,*" remarked the greasy stringy-haired mortician, reciting the salon's popular slogan.

"I'm sorry," said Mully. "But I can't give my card playing buddies here *your* names. I don't know 'em."

"They call my buddy here, Gabey Cutshaw," I said, then held the lamp to keep it from swinging. "And my name's Reece. Shane Reece."

A long smile carved itself along Mully's meaty face. "So boys, what kind of information are you looking for?"

"You seem to know an awful lot about Clayton Motley . . .," I began.

"It's a subject dear to my heart," Mully said.

"Well, we know Clayton Motley had some

68

partners and that they were buried somewhere here in Fairfield. I need to know where!" Furrowing my brow, I stared him down, finding his eyes even through those now-taped-together amber glasses.

"I'm not in the habit of giving in to demands," said Mully. "It's true, I have a vested interest in Clayton Motley. I know him better than anyone else alive, but you see, I usually *trade* information. That stuff I gave you yesterday . . . that was a freebie. But today, it's different. I'm not gonna give you somethin' for nuthin'."

"So what do you want from us?" Gabe questioned. "Play you a hand of cards for the information?"

"No, that's not gonna solve nuthin'. I cheat," said Mully, then threw his head back and roared. His fellow players turned to look at him, but neither one of them wanted a piece of big Mully. "Nope. There's gotta be *somethin'* you have that I want."

As Mully started dealing the cards, I had a brainstorm.

"How about Clayton Motley himself?"

Mully's head snapped up. He removed his

glasses. "What do you mean, Clayton Motley? His body? Boy, that was never found—"

"It's coming to me. It'll be here any time! I'll tell you when and where to expect it." With one hundred percent of the truth on my side, it was easy to bluff.

"If you're offering me the actual remains of Clayton Motley, Mr. Reece, well that is truly worth somethin' to me. But I warn ya, I will be able to tell if it's really him. I know many things."

"I'm sure you do," I said. "I'll be true to my word."

"You make sure that ya are. Cause if you're lyin', I'll come looking for ya, Reece."

Our eyes locked. Neither one of us flinched.

"So," I asked. "Where are those partners buried?"

Mully Sheppard smiled once again and laid down his cards. A royal flush. Very rare. Unless you cheat.

"Rattlesnake Ravine," he said.

# 13

Almost half of Gabe's time was already up. We had to get to the end of the treacherous Rattlesnake Ravine before sundown. The quickest way?

*Horseback.*

Mully Sheppard had not only told us this was the fastest way to get there, but he also loaned me the money to rent the horses. I suppose he figured the remains of Clayton Motley were worth it.

Of course, I didn't have any hard evidence that Motley was really coming at all. Just some bad dreams and a visit from a supernatural spectre. But if it turned out to be true, Mully would be paid back in spades.

Rattlesnake Ravine lay just on the edge of Fairfield, bordering the Dark Woods. It ran at least four miles, winding through jagged rocks and steep cliffs. In the old days, it was a perfect ambush site. Many a stagecoach and wagon train met their end braving what was then the quickest route into Fairfield. The remains of some of those poor souls still reside in the ravine.

At the stable near the mouth of the ravine I met another of Gabe's many cousins, Ned Cutshaw, who had been working there for seven years. Although Gabe had been through the ravine many times (usually at no charge), I'd never been on a horse in my life.

Ned helped us onto a couple of palominos. Gabe's horse had an attitude. It started spinning in circles as soon as he got on, but he reined it in like a pro. As for my horse, it was nice and charming at first, but soon started turning around, bouncing me up and down in the saddle like a paddleball while I begged it to stop. Ned barely managed to stop laughing long enough to calm my horse down.

As Ned led us off into the ravine, he yelled, "REMEMBER, IF IT GETS TOO PAINFUL, JUST SAY *ALTO*, AND THE HORSES WILL STOP!"

Ned's voice faded as we disappeared down the trail.

And man, was it painful.

Not even halfway through, my legs had deadened to the point of amputation, and the muscles in my rear had been numbed into a soupy gelatin. My trust in the horse's sense of direction became the only reason I didn't jump off and walk it on my own. Gabe never once complained, even with me questioning our distance at every turn.

I kept my mind busy by recounting Mully's story about the two partners, Roadie Garnett and Link McCollum.

They had supposedly met up with Clayton in the north.

The two outlaws had been childhood friends. They had grown up breaking laws and pulling pranks together, before crossing over into outright felonies. That sounded familiar. But the two of them soon went on the run, hanging around a town until their wanted posters were tacked up, before moving on. They pulled small jobs together—robbing stores and hijacking stagecoaches—never crossing the line to the next level—cold-blooded murder.

Until they met Clayton Motley.

Garnett and McCollum laid low for awhile,

since most lawmen had a bullet waiting for both of them. They made a good time of it, pillaging traders and small villages for food and trinkets.

Then they tried it in the wrong village.

The small communal tribe had been the object of such attacks before, and was well-prepared when the two grungy cowboys came to rustle the few cattle in the village pens. The tribesmen surprised the outlaws, caught them, and held an impromptu trial. The village medicine man sentenced them to death on the next full moon.

Just days later, before they could be hanged, the village hunters found an injured man in the woods. They brought the man back to the village and treated his wounds. Word spread that the man had been embroiled in a life-and-death battle with the large grizzly bear that lay lifeless beside the dying man. They took him in and saved his life, not realizing that the day he opened his eyes, their fate would be sealed.

They had saved the life of Clayton Motley.

He repaid them by destroying everything.

When he regained his strength, Motley went on a rampage, burning down their village.

In the midst of his tirade, Motley tore open

the cage that held Garnett and McCollum and offered them torches so they could help—the two outlaws accepted the offer gladly. As the village blazed behind them, the three left the snowy north far behind. A gang whose name was to become synonymous with misery. A gang the whole country would fear.

The whole country—except for one man in Fairfield who was trying to make a name for himself.

Great, Great, Great, Great Grandfather Nathaniel pulled off the impossible—putting a bullet into the unstoppable Clayton Motley. However, unknown to most historians (and even Grandpa), Roadie Garnett and Link McCollum did not stick around to avenge their partner. They hopped on to their horses and headed out of town, but Nathaniel chased them down, and caught up with them here in Rattlesnake Ravine.

A shootout ensued, and when the dust settled, Nathaniel was left standing. He buried them here, planting apple tree seeds next to their graves, so that some good might grow out of the evil they had caused.

With great deeds such as that, Nathaniel *should* have made quite a name for himself, yet only a handful of people know his story.

I guess, in the end, although he saved a lot of lives, *killing* never makes you a great person.

As we neared the end of the ravine, I wondered what would happen if things didn't go right. If Clayton Motley *did* return and make good on his promise, how would people remember me?

# 14

We reached the end. A dead, still opening that gave way to the vast countryside beyond Fairfield. Trees blew green in the spring wind, urging us to forget our gruesome task and experience the dappled, reaffirming life found in Mother Nature.

But Gabe had brought a shovel.

And I'd brought a pick.

We had digging to do.

The apple trees still stood at the left edge of the ravine's mouth, just a few feet away from an old, beat-up stagecoach. Miraculously, the old thing looked as if it could still be used. The landowners must have decided to leave it alone, adding authenticity to the old western trail.

"So, we dig at the trees?" asked Gabe.

"At the trees," I replied, wasting no time in hopping off of my steed, Ol' Rearnumber.

We tied our horses to the stagecoach, then stepped slowly over to the apple trees.

An emptiness grew inside me, hollowing my heart, draining my nerves. My emotions wanted out. They wanted no part in what Gabe and I were about to do.

I looked at Gabe.

"Don't look at me," he said. "You first."

I looked down at the snaking roots of the tree; one large spot of dirt screamed for a pick to be driven right through it.

I swallowed, raised my pick above my head, and drove it into the ground.

There. Softer, diggable dirt.

I began.

Gabe moved over to the other tree and forced his shovel into the ground. After the first few jabs, he warmed up to the task.

"So, tell me again. After we dig them out, what do we do?" Gabe asked.

"We find the bullets and pull them out. Those bullets are the only things that will stop Motley."

Gabe looked up at the sinking sun.

"We've got to hurry. I have to be home soon."

"I know, Gabey. Just keep digging!"

"Gabe," he replied, continuing to shovel dirt. "Hey, Shane. Is this wrong?"

*Was he an idiot?* "No, Gabey—it's not wrong at all! As a matter of fact, they're writing up permission slips for our next field trip—AND THIS IS WHAT THEY'RE HOPING OUR PARENTS WILL AGREE TO LET US DO!" Gabe's face drooped, insulted. "Yes, it's wrong. In almost every country. But these are . . . different circumstances, Gabey."

"Gabe," he said, driving his shovel back into the ground—striking something.

I looked over. "Well?"

"I think I've got something," he said.

*The ground underneath me exploded.*

*A bony hand surfaced and grabbed me by the neck. Another emerged and locked around my wrist. The bad one. The one with the pick-ax.*

*Looking down, I saw a body emerging from the dirt.*

**15**

"*THANK YOU, THANK YOU, THANK YOU!*" A rolling voice shrieked from the rotted head rising from the ground to greet me. "*Freedom is once again mine!*"

"**SHANE!**" Gabe yelled, dropping his shovel. He didn't have time to move before the dirt gave way under him, and a gnarled, flaking hand reached out and grabbed his foot.

The hand pinching my throat reared back and pushed, sending me rolling on my back several feet away.

Twisting my neck to see, I glimpsed the worm-eaten body of an undead man stand upright out of the dirt. Its green, decayed skin hung from its limbs like wet leaves, outlining the bony frame that revealed itself in many places. But in its chest, its caved-in, hollowed chest, shone a bright jade object.  Bullet shaped.

*"I, Link McCollum, thank you.  And now I, Link McCollum, must tear you apart because I haven't eaten in a very, very long time!"*

I backed up, my mind screaming.  Dead men.
Walking dead men.

Gabe screamed in wide-eyed horror as the other monster used him as an anchor to pull itself up from the ground, opening its mouth wide as it vainly attempted to suck sweet air into what was left of its flat, torn lungs.

*"ALIVE! STILL ALIVE!"* it cried.  I could only assume it was Roadie Garnett.  He, too, housed a green hunk of metal in his sunken chest.  Gabe shrieked, kicked, and squirmed, desperately trying to tear away.

Garnett would dig into him at any second.

I had to pull myself together.

I had to think fast.

**"I'M SHANE REECE!  MY GREAT, GREAT, GREAT, GREAT GRANDFATHER PUT YOU DOWN, AND I'LL DO THE SAME IF YOU DON'T LET GO OF ME!"**

The two monsters froze for a moment, their entrails whistling and gurgling.

*"VERY BRAVE OF YOU, SON, BUT YER GREAT, GREAT, GREAT, GREAT GRANDFATHER DIDN'T REALLY GET THE JOB DONE, NOW DID HE?"* hissed Link McCollum as he started coming at me. Roadie bent Gabe over his knee, ready to take a bite out of my friend's throat.

My mind reached for an idea and grabbed gold.

**"IF *I* DON'T GET YOU, CLAYTON MOTLEY WILL! HE'S ALIVE, JUST LIKE YOU! HE'S COMING BACK! HE KNOWS WHAT YOU DID! YOU RAN LIKE COWARDS AND DIDN'T EVEN TRY TO AVENGE HIM! HE'LL KILL YOU AGAIN FOR THAT!"**

This time both of them stopped, and I could swear I saw them tremble.

*"It's time for us to go,"* gurgled Link, as he reached down to his bony feet, picked up a rock, and fired it right at me.

I barely managed to duck in time, the rock flying over my head, bouncing off the larger rocks behind me. Before I could move, Roadie Garnett had launched Gabe into the air. He landed flat on his back.

As I rushed to Gabe's side, the two monsters harnessed the horses to the old, dilapidated stagecoach and forced them to run.

"Gabey! Are you all right?!"

He had the wind knocked out of him, but managed to squeak out a couple of words.

"Get 'em."

The rickety passenger wagon rolled forward, the two ghoulish outlaws steering it back through the ravine.

*Heading back to Fairfield! They MUST be panicking!*

I moved quickly, running after the stagecoach before it could pick up too much speed. The last few feet were the hardest, hopping over rocks, sticks, and even a rattlesnake, in order to make that diving leap . . .

My hands locked onto the stage's back luggage handle, leaving my feet to drag on the ground behind me. *Was this real, or was I in an old 'B' western?*

The coach began taking the turns sharply, coming close to the ravine's dirt walls and jagged rocks. My legs swung out with each turn. I practically crushed my teeth to a powder straining to pull my feet in. I kicked up, trying to get enough reach to lock my heel on the rear axle . . .

Success. I was completely aboard, in a manner of speaking. On the verge of pulling every muscle in my body, I lifted myself up, coming within reach of the top luggage bar. The coach whipped from side to side, making the railing a moving target, but my hand finally locked on to it, and I heaved my way to the top.

A cold, dead hand wrapped around my wrist.

Link. Roadie. One of them, I couldn't tell which, loomed over me, grinning as much as a lipless man could.

*"You're dead!"* he cooed, the emerald glow from his chest illuminating every maggot that squirmed from his face.

**"SO ARE YOU!"** I yelled. **"AGAIN!"**

Launching my hand into his dried, corroded cavity, I yanked the bullet from its hundred year resting place.

The dead outlaw's body went limp. Lifeless. It sailed over the top of me, and was smashed into pieces on the ground rushing below us.

Pulling my way to the top, I peered over to the front of the speeding coach. The second outlaw whipped the reins, screaming for the horses to hurry. Sneaking closer, I reached over, hoping to catch the right angle to thrust my hand into his chest and pull out his furnace.

*But he saw me.*

Yanking back on the reins, he forced the horses to put on their brakes, sending me flying forward.

I landed on my horse's back.

The monster then whipped them back up to speed, and we flew through the twisting course at a suicidal pace.

Leaning up between the horses' heads, I screamed one word.

**"ALTO!"**

Their hooves dug into the ground, stopping us almost instantly.

The undead outlaw flew from his seat—straight at me!

I reached out my hand, spearing him in the chest as he passed over me.

The outlaw's bones crashed into the rocks where the ravine turned just a few yards ahead. They spilled to the ground, and I could still see a faint glow dying in the skeleton's sockets before it fell face down in the dirt.

And in my hand, I held his emerald bullet.

# 16

Returning to the Lookout, I hoped to see the spectre once again.

Gabe and I had left the mess in the ravine and returned the horses. We even got Gabe to the grocery store and home on time. I returned to my house to find Grandpa asleep in the La-Z-Boy, moaning Clayton Motley's name over and over.

My situation felt even more desperate.

I needed guidance. Some assurance that what I had would do the job.

That's why I went back to the Lookout and waited.

Thirty minutes had passed and I hadn't done anything except walk around the clearing, drinking hot chocolate, hoping the mysterious spirit would reappear. The stuff always seemed to calm me down when I was younger, and boy, did I need its soothing power now. Of course, drinking it from Grandpa's thermos bittered the taste, but it was the only clean thing I could find. Plus, Grandpa said it was lucky, and I needed all the luck I could get.

I walked under the overcast night sky, not even moonlight to brighten my path.

Then I thought . . . *light*.

The fire had summoned me before. If I made just a tiny one, perhaps Sheriff Drake wouldn't come hustling up the hill to stamp it out.

I gathered a few twigs and piled them into a small mound, away from the edge of the hill and out of sight.

Now, what to use to light it?

I had never learned the whole sticks-rubbing-together thing. Nor did I have any of Grandpa's matches.

But I did have *two magic bullets*.

I lifted the two pieces of bullet-shaped, glowing green shrapnel from my pocket. Gripping one in each hand, I held them over the wood and banged them together.

*Sparks.*

The sparks exploded and fell to the ground,

igniting the kindling into crackling flames.

I warmed myself over the fire, watchdogging the area for an appearance by the ghost.

As the night wind blew gently through the trees, the rustling leaves drowned out all the other tiny, muffled sounds. The same sounds that had previously warned me of the spectre's presence.

I actually found myself growing worried. For some reason, I needed to see this heartstopping apparition more than anything else in the world.

I needed it to tell me what to do.

My eyes desperately circled the entire hilltop.

Nothing.

Funny, I don't know what made me look up.

# 17

The glowing spectre hovered above my head, looking down on me like a night watchman through his favorite security camera.

"I need your help," I muttered.

The ghostly vision gave a slow nod, then lowered itself to the ground to stand in front of me.

"I have the bullets," I said. "Now what do I do with them?"

Even the spectre marveled at the two luminous projectiles, but when I held them up, its expression changed, and I sensed in its actions . . . *disgust.*

*"Melt them. Use the container."*

No problem there.

Dropping the bullets into the thermos, I

extended it over the fire by running a stick through its handle. They melted almost instantly.

I then pulled the thermos from the flame.

*"Pour the metal down this hole."*

*What?* The phantom stood beside a small, very deep hole in the ground.

"You want me to pour this stuff that I risked my life for into the ground?"

*"Yes."*

Well, I'd asked for guidance, and this is what I got. Against my better judgement, I poured the glowing green liquid into the hole, watching it steam in the night air.

"Now what?" I asked.

*"Now you wait. The earth, Fairfield's earth, will mold it into your perfect weapon."*

"Wait? Wait until when?"

*"Until tomorrow. When morning comes, return to this spot and dig up your weapon. Clayton Motley will return to*

*Fairfield at sundown tomorrow. You will be prepared."*

"But what if I don't know how to use this weapon?"

*"You will. Go home. Be ready."*

Like the steam, the apparition dissipated into the air, leaving me alone in the cold, dark night. My heart sank with the thought of waking the next morning knowing that the day could be my very last.

# 18

Sitting down for breakfast with Grandpa that morning seemed very final. The thought of how the day might end was almost unbearable and not very conducive to a hearty appetite.

"Aren't ya gonna eat yer eggs?" Grandpa asked.

"I'm not that hungry, thanks."

"Yer worried about yer parents coming home tonight, eh? Well, just remember, punishments are temporary if ya learn yer lesson. Why don't ya go out and have a little fun today? What'cha got planned?"

*A very loaded question.*

"I've got no plans," I answered. "Any ideas?"

Grandpa looked at my head while nibbling his bacon. "You might try gettin' a haircut. That'd at least give yer parents one less thing to get on ya about."

True words.

As I watched him chew his bacon and give a smile or a frown to each comment from the mete orologist on *The Weather Channel*, I realized that Grandpa was a pretty smart guy. *Though millions of people won't remember his name or share in his wisdom, I will.* I'll remember everything he tells me, and many of my future deci sions will be based on his smart advice. That's his legacy. That's how he lives on. All Nathaniel ever did was shoot a few guys.

Which brought me back to my current problem: how to survive.

"Just keep telling yerself," said Grandpa, "when this is over, I'll never do those bad things again. *And stick to it.*"

"You're right, Grandpa," I said, getting up from my seat.

"Where ya going? Out and about?"

"Oh, I'm gonna get out and dig up something," I replied.

"Well, keep yer nose clean," he remarked as I headed out the door, then called me back for one more question. "Shane-boy? Have ya seen my thermos?"

*Oh, man. I completely forgot about it.*

"Yeah. Sorry, Grandpa.  I used it last night. I'll return it to you."

"That's all right," he said. "Ya keep it.  Ya might need the luck."

# 19

Plunging my hand into the mouth of the small hole gave me shivers. Images of the day before—the undead outlaw springing up from the ground and grabbing my throat—filled my mind. Or worse yet, I imagined him gripping my arm and pulling me under to suffocate next to its entombed corpse.

I felt various insects crawling up my hand as I reached deeper and deeper. The earth grew cold around my hand, perhaps foreshadowing something unbelievably gory happening to my arm.

Nothing did.

My fingers finally touched . . . *metal*.

Closing my hand around it, I yanked the object out of the cold ground.

A perfect sphere, shaped by some natural

hole in the earth.

Clutching it in my hand, I knew its purpose almost immediately.

A weapon. Ammunition. For a slingshot.

"Just ease back," Gabe advised, watching me hold the slingshot, pulling the band back with my shaky arm. "You'd think you'd never done this before."

"It's my bad arm. I can't keep this thing steady."

I let go of the band, firing the rock at an old soda can sitting on a stump ten yards away. It flew off to the side, missing the can by a mile.

"I'm doomed," I said.

Gabe didn't say anything. After I'd snuck to his window, gotten his attention, and asked to borrow his slingshot, he insisted on defying the odds to help me with a little target practice. He had been hopeful at first, but after twenty tries and twenty misses, I could see him getting worried. Before the accident, Shane Reece never missed. Now, when I needed my delinquent slingshot skills the most, they had abandoned me.

"Are you gonna come with me?" I muttered,

loading up my twenty-first rock.

"I—I don't know. If you hadn't come by my house so early today, there's no way I would have been able to sneak out. My parents practically have me locked up, but if I can get there, I will," said Gabe.

I pulled back the band and let the rock fly.

Another terrible shot zoomed three feet over my target.

I didn't look at Gabe.

I don't know if he looked at me.

## 20

I, Shane Reece, hereby leave the following:

To my friend, Gabe, I give any of my earthly possessions that you deem cool or useful. May you take advantage of these tools, put yourself on the right track, and stop getting into trouble all of the time. You probably won't have a big problem doing so, now that I'm not around to talk you into doing bad things.

To my parents I leave my love, because once Gabe has all of my stuff, that's all I have to give. I'd like you to remember me as a kid who, in the end, did the right thing and tried to prevent trouble rather than start it. I'll miss you both.

Finally, to Grandpa, I leave you your own thermos. It obviously didn't bring me the luck we wished. Please know that I respected you and wish I'd spent more time getting to know you. In *my last moments, your words were the ones I held closest to my heart. I'll miss you all, and if I had one wish, it would be to be with you all once again.*

*Your friend, son, and grandson,*
*Shane Reece*

I rolled up the will, tied a ribbon around it, and placed it on my desk.

Three o'clock in the afternoon.

Almost time.

I'd never been into Lloyd Phillips' barber shop before. But today it seemed almost . . . appropriate.

"So, have we had it with the Hair Conquistador?" Lloyd asked, cleaning his scissors with an old rag.

"It just didn't feel right going there today," I told him, plopping myself down into his red-leather barber chair.

Except for the guy sitting in the other chair with his face buried in the newspaper, I seemed to be his only customer. The man lowered the *Fairfield Gazette* and I saw the section he was reading.

The obituaries.

Before Lloyd could trim them off, the hairs on the back of my neck rose.

The man behind the paper was John Cratchett—town mortician.

"Well," he said, "fancy meeting you here."

"Just getting my hair cut," I dead-panned.

"What kind of cut do you want, kid?" asked Lloyd.

"Make it look good. Whatever it takes," I told him. "And I'd also like a shave."

"Son, you're too young to shave. Why don't you wait a few years?"

"Because you never know when you've got a few years. I want to get my shave in while I know I can."

I knew they both noticed my agitation.

"So, son, are you still keeping that crazy promise you made to Mully Sheppard?" asked John Cratchett.

"Yeah. I'm gonna try to make good on it today."

"You're gonna face down Clayton Motley? Boy, living or dead, that man's a force of nature, a killing machine. You get close to him and nothing good can come of it," warned Lloyd while lathering my face.

I heard a sliding noise and looked to my side to find John Cratchett measuring my arm with a tape measure. Then he measured my legs.

"What are you doing?" I asked, getting a little angry.

"Well, if you're gettin' involved with Clayton Motley, I'm going to be getting some business," said the town mortician. "Just getting a head start on it, that's all."

Great.

Using the smock stretched over me, I stuck my face into its fabric, wiping off the shaving lather.

"What's the problem, son?" asked Lloyd.

"Everybody's talking in my ear. Clayton Motley's bad. Clayton Motley's the meanest man on Earth. Well, I'm sick of it. No one knows what's going to happen. No one can predict the future, but everyone thinks they know better than me because up 'til two days ago, I'd never heard of Clayton Motley! But you know what? *He's in trouble too.* 'Cause Clayton Motley's never heard of *me!*"

With that, I crashed out the doors, on my way to Blood Creek.

**21**

Sundown.

Sundown at Blood Creek.

The creek had been forgotten over the years. The highway that ran over it received the same amount of attention.

I'd been standing on the deserted road for two minutes, watching the road. The old highway dipped out of sight about half a mile away. The sun was setting behind it, so with my hand over my eyes, I struggled to make out a figure or distinguish some form of movement.

Nothing.

But he'd be coming from that way.

I knew it.

I walked over the two lane road, grass growing through its veiny cracks. Kicking up chunks of old faded asphalt, I made my way over to the bridge and looked over.

Black water. Dense, threaded moss floated on its surface, an undisturbed skin that keeps you guessing as to the depth of the slowly churning pool.

The sides of the road had been taken over by wild vegetation, but some things could still be seen. Old shacks and a small abandoned grocery stood almost hidden behind the hanging brush. An antique gas pump, standing alone in the plant life, looked almost comically out of place with its round, white header simply reading *Gas*. A reminder that this road had once been traveled a great deal. That people probably stood exactly where I was now, fishing and catching up on the town gossip.

That had been some time ago.

Now the only thing Blood Creek had to offer was a resounding sense of doom. Even the trees whispered promises of misery as they blew in the wind. I got the feeling that if I perished here the land would swallow me, cover me with moss, and let the world forget about me.

If I made it out alive, I'd never come back to Blood Creek.

And why was I there?

The visions. The visions of Clayton Motley hunting me down, never giving up until he'd gunned down every last Reece.

I had no help. No one would believe my story except Gabe. Unfortunately, my sidekick had other things to do.

There was always the spectre. I'd swallowed everything that spook had spouted. I secretly hoped the ghost had fed me a line of garbage, or that his facts were all wrong.

I'd soon find out.

*Don't be afraid. Keep your mind busy.*

Reaching down, I picked up a rock and slapped it into the slingshot, pulled back and aimed at my target.

The old gas pump.

I had ol' *Gas* right in my sights, but when I let the rock go I assumed that it could have only been a cosmic act that caused my shooting to grow so poor. I didn't even come close.

*I am soooooo dead . . .*

*I should try again.*

Scavenging the ground for a good rock, I spotted one on the other side of the road. A speckled, shiny piece of granite. Great slingshot ammunition. I walked over and scooped it up, feeling its perfect weight in the center of my hand.

*With this one, I can't miss,* I thought, glancing toward the setting sun.

*Someone was standing at the end of the road.*

Shock. Instant shock. My body convulsed with multiple nervous reactions: my heart leaping through my chest; the muscles in my throat locking themselves, squeezing the air from my lungs; my hands turning to pillows; my legs to straw; a single message pounding in my head—run, RUN, **RUN!**

But I wobbled, a miserable excuse for the sharp tack I'd been seconds before.

The figure stood at the horizon, unmoving. A cold monolith emanating terror.

The wind grew stronger, picking up the dirt and the dead grass crammed within the highway cracks. I felt it crawling over me, searching. Then I heard words, floating over the gusts like surfers on a wave.

"ARE YOU ANOTHER REECE?"

The voice. Ice-chilled, sounding like a bag of shattered glass asking questions.

"Shane Reece," I said.

The wind died slightly, framing his next word . . .

## "DRAW."

# 22

My hands shook uncontrollably, hanging by my sides, searching for a bazooka, a Patriot missile—anything with more fire power than what I had.

I'd never hit him at that range.

I knew the slightest move would set him off. Any mistaken effort to go for my weapon and he'd fill me full of lead.

*If only he would come closer.*

Again the evil shadow spoke.

## "DRAW."

Until I made a move, nothing would happen.

*Hey, I can stand here all day. All year if I have to.*

Then I felt the deadliest words float gently

to my ear.

Oh, no. That's it. I'm finished.

I gave one final call for my nerves to steady themselves and for my eyes to dry and focus themselves on their target.

My glowing, green ammo lay ready in my shirt pocket.

I'd have to be fast. Faster than I had ever been before.

Now.

*Shooting my hand into my pocket, I yanked out the green ball, slapped it into the band of my slingshot, and let it fly.*

It was a pathetic attempt.

The ball (which had not been loaded perfectly) popped into the air, bounced off one of the thousands of cracks in the road, and soared over the side of the bridge to splash in the dreary water below.

A mad, cackling roared from the end of the road. I saw the dark figure raise his guns, then I heard two blasts, so close together they were almost one.

Fireballs.

Fireballs streaming from his six-shooters instead of bullets. Coming my way.

I didn't waste any time in scrambling to the side of the road, just before the projectiles exploded behind me. Asphalt erupted into the air, sending bits of road showering down on me as I bolted into the brush. I ran over bushes, trampled small trees, and tore through gates of briar vines before coming to the old forgotten store.

The door practically came off in my hand when I pulled it open. It felt rotted from the inside out, probably hollowed years before by an army of termites. Accidentally unhinging it at the top, I tried bringing the slab of wood shut once I got inside—but it'd grown tired of standing. It came off its frame and fell to the ground with a loud slap.

I ducked inside, losing myself in the shadows.

Hundreds of potential dangers raced through my mind. Rats. Snakes. Large spiders. Sharp, rusted cans or shards of glass poking straight up from the floor.

But that was kiddie stuff compared to what was outside.

I waited.

Watching the road nervously, I heard something in the distance. A clanging sound. No, a jingle. Soft at first, it began to resonate over the waters of the creek, growing louder by the second until it tightened my heart and chased the air from my chest.

Spurs. Jingling with every step the monster took. Coming closer.

Suddenly, Clayton Motley came into full view. He passed the trees that had obscured my vision of him and walked over the bridge. Once he crossed it he stopped . . .

*And looked my way.*

Shuddering, my eyes washed over the horror that had killed me so many times before in my nightmares.

The worn, rickety terror that was Clayton Motley. The dried, green corpse. A skull with sunken sockets, still with some meat still dangling from his cheeks and under his chin. The ripped Stetson riddled with holes, and filled with crawling worms. A long coat hung from his frame like the cape of a king, covered in filth, mildew, and other growing fungi. His boots were simply black, but shiny and stiff with age.

Standing solemnly on the deserted road, peering into the old store for his prey, the undead outlaw struck a terrifying chord as the sun set gently behind him.

Darkness fell, and Clayton Motley came my way.

A horrible, sweating panic washed over me. I'd trapped myself. This merciless killer was stalking his way to my rotted hiding place, *and I had completely trapped myself.*

But I still had my slingshot.

In a frenzy, I searched the ground under me to find one rock to launch—one piece of scrap that might buy me a precious few seconds.

I felt metal. An old hunk of rusted metal. Sharp. A tetanus shot waiting to happen. I held it tightly in the sling band, sharp side out like an arrow waiting to be fired.

The rustling outside grew louder and the walking dead-man emerged from the brush.

Trembling. My hand. My arm. My entire body. Trembling. As the terror's shadow passed in front of the doorway and his form filled its void, I knew that if I missed this shot, I wouldn't get another chance.

The monster entered, guns literally blazing.

They lit up the darkened interior, revealing the secret lying low in the far corner.

*Me.*

I let the metal fly.

*Thwack! A perfect shot. The shrapnel stuck in his forehead, sending his neck snapping backward.*

I moved quickly, heading out one of the glassless front windows as Motley's guns lit up brightly, spraying multiple shots of balled flame into the store. The place went up like a book of matches.

I hit the ground running. Less than two steps later a fireball passed me, striking a tree just a few yards away.

The outlaw was right behind me.

I tore through the brush until the ground beneath me became mush and my feet began to bog down in the mire.

Before I knew it, I'd trapped myself again. Directly in front of me—Blood Creek.

*Nowhere to run.*

# 23

Footsteps crashed through the bushes and limbs, then stopped right behind me.

Clayton Motley pointed his fire-spitting six-shooter directly at me.

My feet kicked back, running me backwards into the creek. The first step was all mud, the second all water. I fell through the mossy skin on top, right into the cold, black filth underneath.

I kicked my feet helplessly, unable to find the bottom, then I pulled myself back up to the surface.

Motley gave a long curdling growl and stepped forward, cocking his pistol, set to blast me away.

I floated helplessly in front of him. Nowhere to go. He had me dead-to-rights. As he pointed his weapon at me, I stared into his empty black sockets, looking for mercy. To say something. *Anything!*

**"HEAD DOWN, KID!"** Someone screamed.

Another figure leaped out of the brush to tackle Clayton Motley, sending them both crashing into the water. When they sprang up, wrestling like madmen, I saw who it was.

*Mully Sheppard.*

He'd saved me. Or did he?

Clayton held him at bay with one hand and took aim at me with the other.

**"GO UNDER, KID!  GO UNDER!"** yelled Mully, struggling to free himself from Clayton's grip.

As the gun's barrel burst with a brilliant burning light, I ducked into the diseased blackness, swimming away from the battle. I felt the blast strike the top of the water just above me, and could see the entire surface ignite into flame. Grungy, old flammable creek.

I held my breath, searching for a spot to surface, but the entire creek had lit up, and I could feel the cold water growing warmer.

My air was thinning. My eyes hurt from the various algae and junk that drifted menacingly through the dark waters. Finding a spot to breathe seemed hopeless until finally I swam past the flames. Shooting up from the water, I turned quickly to see if Mully had won the fight.

He was nowhere to be seen.

Only the figure of Clayton Motley moved toward me through the flames, gun extended, ready to wipe me off the face of the earth.

He fired.

I took another breath and ducked under.

Again, the surface of the water burst into flames. I knew my only chance was to outswim it once again, emerge, and hopefully have enough time to clamber out of the creek.

So I kept swimming.

Unfortunately, Clayton kept firing, further igniting the creek and insuring my doom. I couldn't swim far enough ahead.

My breath had run out.

My vision started to dim.

My arms and legs slowed.

The water grew cold once again.

Though the flames lit my way underwater, blackness started clouding in around me.

I was going to drown.

Then I spotted something. Something in the distance.

**24**

I sprang from the water, gasping for air.

But I was ready.

I'd found an opening in the flames. Maybe a foot in diameter, but still an opening.

And it wasn't the only thing I'd found.

Pulling back the band on my slingshot, I held the strange, green ball—ready to fire.

The flames licked close to my face, attempting to obscure my vision of the walking terror behind them.

Once he saw me, Clayton Motley started laughing again. He held his guns out in front of him, cocking both simultaneously. Wading through the flames, his cackling grew louder. He came closer. Closer.

I let the ball fly.

It shot through the air, striking Motley in

the chest. His cackling stopped. His screaming began. Green electrical sparks shot out from his quaking body. The water around him bubbled to a boil. The flames sucked back, clinging to him as if his bones were kindling. He howled, pulling the triggers on his guns.

Fireballs streamed through the air.

No time to duck.

The flaming projectiles soared past me on both sides, exploding into trees on each side of the creek, bursting them into flames.

Clayton Motley was still screaming, glowing a bright green that slowly started melting his bones. He drooped and spilled over into the burning pool.

Then he dissipated, his jade-lit bones drifting apart and floating down the creek.

His guns sank. His coat went under, too.

His burning hat, however, drifted my way before finally submerging with a bubbling hiss.

Mully Sheppard had taken quite a beating. While I was underwater, Clayton Motley had launched him up into the trees. He crashed down at the side of the creek, completely unconscious.

But he was half-awake when I found him. I told him about Clayton and he said . . .

"Let the creek have him. He was too much for me. But I guess he wasn't more than you could handle, eh?"

"Why, Mr. Sheppard? Why did you show up?" I asked.

"I had to see if you were on the up and up. I've lived with the legacy of Clayton Motley for a long time. Putting him to rest was very important to me."

"Legacy?"

"Clayton Motley . . ." announced Mully, " . . . is my great, great, great grandfather. He scarred my ancestry, shaming my family for generations, and the legends of his return always kept the talk alive. I wanted to find his remains and bury him once and for all. Today, you've helped me do that."

"You're much obliged," I told him, sounding again like the hero from some corny old western.

"Thank ya, son. Now if you don't mind, my truck's just up the ways a little, parked off the road. I might need your help with the first steps there."

I steadied Mully through the brush. He felt heavier than he looked, and I was glad to see he didn't need any further help from me once we got to the road.

"I was going to leave for Mullinfield tonight—for the Earthquake Relief Benefit Show—but with all the excitement, I left my best songs written on a handkerchief in my hotel room, so I have to go back into town—do you need a lift?" he asked, as a familiar wind began to blow through the trees.

A signal.

A signal letting me know that someone else might want a word with me.

"It's cool," I told him. "I think I'm going to walk. I've got . . . people to see."

"All right, pardner. Just get in before it gets too late, y'know. Your parents will worry!"

"Will do!" I exclaimed, and waved to Mully as he trudged up the road to his awaiting truck.

My parents. They'd be home any time now. I'd have to get home before—

I saw the lily-white face of the spectre leering at me from the brush. As I heard Mully's engine start up from down the road, I watched the ghost's finger signaling me forward.

"It's over," I said. "Clayton Motley is finished. You should be able to rest in peace now."

Again, it beckoned me over.

Mully's truck pulled into the road and headed into town, honking its horn at me as it departed. I watched its lights disappear, suddenly wishing I'd taken Mully up on his offer.

I warily made my way over to the glowing face that stared at me so coldly, so . . . unhappily.

"WHO ARE YOU?" I asked, as I approached its floating form.

*"I think you know."*

"N-Nathaniel? Nathaniel Reece?"

The spectre nodded.

"I knew it. I mean, I didn't really know, but it all makes sense now. Well, you can rest in peace now. I've finished your unfinished business, and now that I know about your historic gunfight, I can pass the word. I can make sure your name becomes *legend*."

The spectre shook his head, then . . .

*"My actions were not legendary. They were acts of greed and desperation. I wanted my name to go down in history, even if it meant dabbling in the unknown and killing three men. In the end, no one remembers me and the tools I used to make my mark carried a curse that has haunted my descendants for generations. Please, Shane Reece, learn from my mistakes—they're going to cost you!"*

"Me? No, I'm fine. I mean, I was scared facing Motley and all, but I came out of it okay! I'm still going to be in pretty deep trouble when my parents get back, but I know I deserve it! This—this has taught me a lesson. No more crazy stunts for me. I've got to accept some responsibility—just like Grandpa wants me to. I've got to respect authority—I've got to make Mom and Pop proud . . ."

*"Shane, there is something you have to know—"*

"SHANE!"

I whipped around, looking down the road to

find Gabe flying my way on his bicycle, pumping his brakes to stop.

The spirit of Nathaniel Reece disappeared in front of me as Gabe slid to a stop, spraying loose gravel into the air.

"WH—WHAT ARE YOU DOING HERE?" I asked.

"I had to come! I couldn't let my partner face this thing alone! Where is he?"

"It's over," I said. "The good guys won."

"YOU SAW HIM? HE WAS ACTUALLY HERE?! DID HE LOOK LIKE THE THINGS WE DUG UP YESTERDAY? IS HE DEAD—?"

"It's over, Gabey."

Gabe bit his lip and decided to keep his questions for later.

"Listen," he said, "we'd better get back. I think this adventure has already cost us plenty. As is, we're never going to be able to leave our homes again."

Looking over my shoulder, I searched for the spectre's face, looking for the ghost of my great, great, great, great grandfather to appear and give me some parting words of wisdom.

But he never showed.

"You're right. Let's go. Mom and Pop will be

home shortly," I said. "Anyway, my job here's done."

I hopped on the bike with Gabe, and we slowly made our way down the road, riding off into the sunset, eyes wide open to our next adventure.

The spectre of Nathaniel Reece reappeared.

*"Someday, Shane,"* remarked the spectre, *"Someday I'll tell you what happened to the other three bullets in that six-shooter of mine, and maybe then, you can prove that your name really is worthy of legend . . ."*

# About the Authors

**Marty M. Engle** and **Johnny Ray Barnes Jr.**, graduates of the Art Institute of Atlanta, are the creators, writers, designers and illustrators of the **Strange Matter**™ series and the **Strange Matter**™ World Wide Web page.

Their interests and expertise range from state of the art 3-D computer graphics and interactive multi-media, to books and scripts (television and motion picture).

Marty lives in La Jolla, California with his wife Jana and twin terror pets, Polly and Oreo.

Johnny Ray lives in Tierrasanta, California and spends every free moment with his fiancée, Meredith.

# And now
# an exciting preview
# of the next

## #17 Tune In To Terror

## by Marty Engle

# 1

Billy Keen's eyes hadn't moved for the last five minutes. He couldn't allow them to. Not even for a moment. The strain of trying to remain motionless began taking its toll. Small tremors of terror traveled the length of his eleven-year-old body, delivering cramps, aches, and pains all along the way. His lower lip quivered, his heart pounded. The buzzing in his head fogged his thinking—*but not his fear.*

He stared intently over the edge of the metal crate he had crouched behind and down the metal-framed corridor lined with pipes and crossbeams. The long skinny lights above him dimmed and flickered erratically, hissing and spitting like angry hornets.

*Nothing yet. No sign of movement at the entrance of the hallway.*

He dared not blink or breathe or even

move a muscle. He knew that the slightest sign of life was all it needed to find him.

*Billy was hiding from doom.*

He imagined this doom to be about ten feet tall, stalking the maze of corridors with machine-like precision and glowing-red eyes.

He hadn't actually *seen* his pursuer, only its shadow, but that was enough to freeze his blood and send him fleeing in a silent panic, gulping down the screams as fast as they rose in his throat.

*He neglected to notice that he had run down a dead-end corridor.* No way out.

Hiding behind the stack of metal crates against the back wall, he watched intently for the inevitable shadow to fall upon the corridor floor. Waited for the monstrous form to step into the entryway. Dreaded his first good look at the horror that was coming for him.

Billy ducked behind the crates and bit his lip to keep from screaming. Tears ran from his wide staring eyes.

*Was that its shadow he saw?*

His heartbeat quickened and his breath grew short. His mind raced with flashing thoughts of escape—but there was none.

*He would have to fight—but how?*

*Billy Keen didn't notice the panel sliding silently open behind him. Didn't see the two, large mechanical claws stretching and spreading toward him like hideous cranes from the darkness. Couldn't feel the razor-sharp talons closing in on his neck and over his head.*

*Billy could only shriek when the claws pulled him back into the darkness.*

"AW MAN!" Billy yelled, shoving the keyboard away. He threw his hands in the air with a defeated moan. "I almost had him that time!"

On the computer screen in front of him, the words—GAME OVER.

He jerked back in his chair, nearly hitting the small blonde girl with wire-frame glasses sitting beside him. "WHAT?! Get over it. He had you so trapped, there was no WAY you could have gotten out. You were hopelessly smeared," Sara said, laughing at Billy's eighth brutal defeat of the evening.

"She's right," Kevin agreed, squinting his eyes, leaning back in his chair, and locking his hands behind his head. He stared at the screen analytically. His ten-year-old mind raced, searching for a strategy Billy could have used in that particular scenario. The conclusion—"Nope. He had you. You couldn't have won."

Sara smiled at Billy and nudged him playfully. "Face it. No one can beat him—not even me."

Sara wasn't kidding. She was arguably the best video-game player of the group. Kevin could gracefully admit to her superior skill, but not Billy.

Billy fixed her with a freezing stare.

"Just wait," he sneered, pulling his chair defiantly up to the desk.

The room was dark and cluttered, littered with piles of empty soda cans, empty cheese puffs bags, and stacks of video game cartridges. The curtains were closed and the lights were dim.

One wall was covered with video game posters yanked from magazines and homemade computer-graphics printouts.

Most prominent, however, was a large write-on/wipe-off scoreboard, obviously well used. Ghostly images of scores from weeks back still lingered below the fresh ones. It hung below a poster of the Bloodinator Cyborg (from the popular movie series of the same name).

The board had about fourteen names listed out. Among them were his own (Billy Keen), Kevin Chandler, and Sara White, his two best friends and video game addicts. At the top of the board was the name of their game, *Nexus— Virtual Reality With A Bite.*

Nexus was the hottest on-line computer game around, a type of multi-player modem game in which players from bedrooms and basements all over the country would enter the same maze-like virtual world to run, fight—*or die.*

Tension, excitement, and massive disappointment filled each virtual warrior's room at different times, depending on what was happening on their computer screen.

"C'mon, Sara. We have to get going," Kevin said, nodding toward Billy. "Mr. Dies-A-Lot will be here all night. It's almost dinnertime."

Kevin rose from the chair he had been planted in for the better part of three hours and stretched his back. Sara sprang from her seat, squinted, and pinched the bridge of her nose under her glasses.

All three kids groaned and exhaled deeply, weary from their latest marathon. Their eyes were stinging and watery, glazed-over from video glare.

"Wait! Where are you guys going? I'm just getting warmed up! I'm going to take him this time. You wait . . . c'mon," Billy exclaimed.

They both shook their heads and sighed. They had seen him like this before. Staring eyes, sweaty face, shaky hands, squeaky, excited voice. It would be hours before he would come out of it. Kevin called it 'Nexus-mode', after the on-line computer game that had his friend hopelessly addicted.

In particular, Billy's mania involved defeating the current reigning champion, the mysterious player who went by the on-line name of BloodinatorX. No one could beat him. His skills were incomparable, as Billy had discovered again and again.

"See you later, Billy," Sara called back.

"Later, pal," Kevin echoed.

They both looked back at the small round boy, his blonde hair lit from the glow of the screen, his face within inches of the monitor. They could tell he had already given up on them and was sinking back into the virtual world of Nexus.

"Get some sun, Billy," Kevin said as he closed the door.

"Fine. Leave. I don't care," Billy mumbled, mentally preparing for the next round. He wouldn't stop. He could *beat* BloodinatorX tonight. He just knew it. *He could feel it.* All he had to do was keep playing, keep going. Tonight would be the night. No doubt about it.

Billy paced the room a bit, closed his eyes, and recalled as many maps and strategies as he could. He took another swallow of cola, ate another handful of cheese puffs for strength, and sat down to do battle.

His finger reached for the 'return' key, the key that would send him spiraling into another virtual battle against enemies he had never actually met—or *would soon wish he'd never met.*

*With just one press of the key, Billy was about to launch himself into a nightmare he could not possibly have imagined.*

# Introducing

STRANGERS ™

## An incredible new club exclusively for readers of Strange Matter™

To receive exclusive information on joining this *strange* new organization, simply fill out the slip below and mail to:

STRANGE MATTER INFO •Front Line Art Publishing • 9808 Waples St. • San Diego, California 92121

Name _____ Age _____

Address _____

City _____ State _____ Zip _____

How did you hear about Strange Matter™? _____

_____

What other series do you read? _____

_____

Where did you get this Strange Matter™ book? _____

_____

# THE SCARIEST PLACE IN CYBERSPACE.

Visit STRANGE MATTER™ on the
World Wide Web at
http://www.strangematter.com

for the latest news, fan club information,
contests, cool graphics,
strange downloads and more!

# CONTINUE THE ADVENTURE...

with the StrangeMatter™ library.
Experience a terrifying new
StrangeMatter™ adventure every month.

#1 No Substitutions
#2 Midnight Game
#3 Driven to Death
#4 A Place to Hide
#5 The Last One In
#6 Bad Circuits
#7 Fly the Unfriendly Skies

#8 Frozen Dinners
#9 Deadly Delivery
#10 Knightmare
#11 Something Rotten
#12 Dead On Its Tracks
#13 Toy Trouble
#14 Plant People
#15 Creature Features

Available where you buy books.

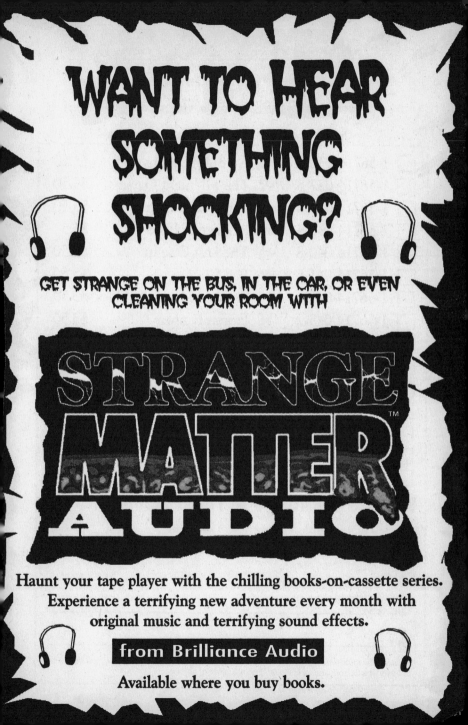

# STRANGE MATTER™

Order now or take this page to your local bookstore!

| | | | | |
|---|---|---|---|---|
| ☐ | 1-56714-036-X | #1 | No Substitutions | $3.50 |
| ☐ | 1-56714-037-8 | #2 | The Midnight Game | $3.50 |
| ☐ | 1-56714-038-6 | #3 | Driven to Death | $3.50 |
| ☐ | 1-56714-039-4 | #4 | A Place to Hide | $3.50 |
| ☐ | 1-56714-040-8 | #5 | The Last One In | $3.50 |
| ☐ | 1-56714-041-6 | #6 | Bad Circuits | $3.50 |
| ☐ | 1-56714-042-4 | #7 | Fly the Unfriendly Skies | $3.50 |
| ☐ | 1-56714-043-2 | #8 | Frozen Dinners | $3.50 |
| ☐ | 1-56714-044-0 | #9 | Deadly Delivery | $3.50 |
| ☐ | 1-56714-045-9 | #10 | Knightmare | $3.50 |
| ☐ | 1-56714-046-7 | #11 | Something Rotten | $3.50 |
| ☐ | 1-56714-047-5 | #12 | Dead On Its Tracks | $3.50 |
| ☐ | 1-56714-052-1 | #13 | Toy Trouble | $3.50 |
| ☐ | 1-56714-053-x | #14 | Plant People | $3.50 |
| ☐ | 1-56714-054-8 | #15 | Creature Features | $3.50 |

## I'M A STRANGE MATTER™ ZOMBIE!

Please send me the books I have checked above. I am enclosing $_____ (please add $2.00 to cover shipping and handling). Send check or money order to Montage Publications, 9808 Waples Street, San Diego, California 92121 - no cash or C.O.D.'s please.

NAME _____ AGE_____

ADDRESS_____

CITY_____ STATE _____ ZIP_____

Please allow four to six weeks for delivery. Offer good in the U.S. only. Sorry, mail orders are not available to residents of Canada. Prices subject to change.